The Purple Culture

The Purple Culture

A NOVEL

STEPHEN BOEHRER

Oceanview Publishing
IPSWICH, MASSACHUSETTS

ISBN: 978-1-933515-24-3

Published in the United States of America by Oceanview Publishing,
Ipswich, Massachusetts
www.oceanviewpub.com

10 9 8 7 6 5 4 3 2 1

PRINTED IN THE UNITED STATES OF AMERICA

To Judy Bridges of Redbird Studio in Milwaukee
for the Craft
and
To Alana Lennie of Lennie Literary Agency
for her faith in the project.

My thanks to my dedicated and brutally honest
readers: Rita B., Renee R., Terry R., Barbara H.,
Kate S., Rita and Jim M., Mary Ann and Jack M.,
Clare and Paul S., Betty R., and Jane F.

The Purple Culture

Chapter One

His mind on potential defense strategies, James Kobs drove from home to office by habit, flowing with the heavy traffic, obeying lights, and parking in his reserved spot. He walked into the law firm lobby so absorbed in thought the words "Kobs, Mayer, and Guggenbuhl," spoken by the receptionist into her headset, failed to penetrate his concentration. Nor did stooping to straighten an out-of-alignment Persian runner or an automatic and perfunctory inspection of the waiting area stop his introspection.

Kobs walked down an office-lined corridor and turned into the library. He pulled a book from a shelf and snugged his large frame into one of the carrels. *Damn*, he thought, *they designed these carrels for midgets.*

"I've been trailing you," a feminine voice said. "Is that *Legal Ethics 101* in your hands?" Marcie Frederick's blonde hair and pretty face appeared above the carrel's front panel. Tease beamed from the associate attorney's eyes.

Kobs held the book up for inspection.

Marcie peeled the foil off a mint taken from the reception desk. *"Thought Reform and the Psychology of Totalism — A Study of Brainwashing in China* by Robert Jay Lifton. Why do I suddenly feel a chill? Are you planning a Chinese thought implant for David and me?"

Kobs laughed. "I wouldn't have a chance, Marcie. You both have impregnable minds. No, I'm interested to see if an insanity defense lurks in here somewhere. What do you think?"

"I've never gone beyond standard psychological concepts."

Kobs hauled his large six two body erect. "Get David, please, and meet me in my office."

Ten minutes later, Marcie rejoined Kobs in his spacious office, David Crane in tow. David, tall and gangly with lopsided features, was Kobs's other associate. The pair took seats opposite their boss at his conference table.

Kobs handed a slip of paper across the conference table. "You ever hear of these guys?" He stroked his red stubble beard and waited.

They read the names. Both responded, "No."

"They're Roman Catholic bishops," Kobs said. "They have an appointment with me at three tomorrow afternoon. Cliff Hayes of Hayes, Russell, and Hayes made the appointment."

"Hayes is corporate law, isn't he? What's it about?" David asked.

"Don't know for sure. He mentioned an ongoing grand-jury investigation. No indictment yet. I don't know if its federal or not, but Bill Goulding, our estimable assistant U.S. attorney, had a special grand jury convened some months ago. That's all I know at this time. I want you two to check those guys out. Find out what you can. We'll meet on it at eleven tomorrow."

"I'm in court at eleven," David said. "Should be out by noon though."

"Does one work?" Kobs asked.

David nodded.

"Works for me," Marcie said

"If you get time, sniff out the federal courthouse. Maybe you can get something on this grand jury."

Marcie was in Kobs's office at twelve fifty-five the next day. She sat silent at the table reviewing her notes.

Kobs sat at his desk looking at Marcie. That face is the perfect camouflage, he thought, recalling the day he interviewed her for the job. His first impression told him she didn't have a chance. He'd be polite and go through the motions. She had a guileless expression. *Pert and pretty, but she's not bright enough*, he'd thought. But, responding to his questions, she'd displayed a legal knowledge beyond her years of experience, tight reasoning, and a powerful imagination. It was the perfect combination for a criminal defense attorney. He'd hired her on the spot and never regretted it. Lucky me, he thought. When David's frame and face appeared in the doorway, Kobs moved to the table.

Marcie began her report: "Robert Courteer is bishop of San Miguel, Texas. Vincent Barieno is bishop of Palm Sands, Florida, and Wilbur Sandes is bishop of Colchester, New Hampshire. They sped rapidly up the career ladder, making bishop in their forties. All three are originally from the Chicago archdiocese, proteges of retired Cardinal Brendan Patrick O'Connell himself. O'Connell had sent all three to Rome for their four years of theology studies prior to their ordinations, and again later for advanced specialty degrees. All very bright guys, or so I'm told. That's all I've got so far."

"David?" Kobs asked.

"I got practically nothing at the courthouse," David said. "A secretary over there — I once dated her — told me she heard in the lunchroom it had to do with sexual abuse of minors. Goulding really has the security lid on this one."

"We'll just have to wait and see," Kobs replied.

David escorted the four men from the reception room to a conference room adorned elegantly with a polished, oval walnut table, leather chairs, and original art. A portrait, *Guggenbuhl-at-Trial* loomed from the wall. He offered freshly brewed coffee from a ceramic pot on the walnut server and poured for the two takers.

Jim Kobs and Marcie entered the room. Kobs's eyes moved from face to face in assessment. His smile was cordial, his eyes cool.

Attorney Cliff Hayes, a short man with an officious air, handled the introductions of the three bishops.

Kobs shook their hands, testing their grip and their eyes. He introduced Marcie and David and motioned to the chairs. Once seated, Kobs took in the three bishops again, putting to memory their names and their appearances. All three were in clerical garb. Bishop Barieno was tall and hefty, but not fat. He was bald and wore glasses. Impressive in looks and posture, he wore a smile comfortably. Bishop Sandes was of medium height, perhaps five ten, overweight and fleshy, with a puffed face. He, too, wore glasses and had gray hair, combed straight back. He appeared serious and slightly withdrawn. Bishop Courteer was thin and austere looking. He had gray eyes and pallor. He also wore glasses. His face hid any emotion and concealed his thinking.

"How can we help you gentlemen?" Kobs asked.

"There's a grand jury —" Hayes began.

Bishop Sandes, heavy faced, cut him off. "Attorney Hayes has recommended you to us," he said, his tone affected and oracular. "We came to check you out."

"Really!" Kobs's tone was deferential. "Do you know a great deal about criminal law, sir?"

"Of course not. We came to assess you as a person."

Kobs's voice chilled slightly. "What does that mean, sir? You want to know if I'm likeable, or tractable?"

"Something like that."

"And what exactly are your criteria for likeable and tractable?"

"Ah, I don't know exactly. It's a matter of discernment, personal taste if you like."

Kobs stared at Sandes. "I see. Be kind enough to let me instruct you here. You hire a criminal defense attorney for only two reasons. Either to keep you from being indicted, or once indicted, to keep you out of jail. You want to hire someone with the requisite skill to do that, if doing that is at all possible. You don't have to like your attorney. And your attorney doesn't have to like you. From a legal success standpoint, liking each other is at best irrelevant. In fact it may well work to your advantage if the opposite is true. Your time can be spent responding to your attorney's need for accurate information. And the attorney can center on the facts and on defense strategy. So, if you want to judge me, I suggest you do so on my record. Cliff can inform you on that."

"You don't like Catholics?" Bishop Barieno asked, slightly jovial.

"I am a Catholic. That is irrelevant here."

"You don't like bishops?" Barieno again, putting on a winning smile.

"I don't know you three men as individuals," Kobs replied calmly. "I may or may not like you if I did. As a collective, I find the hierarchy unimpressive at best." He turned to Hayes. "Cliff, what's this all about?"

"There is a grand jury in session with an indictment presented to them by Assistant U.S. Attorney William Goulding. I suspect the indictment alleges that these good bishops have been guilty of protecting pedophiles."

"How long have you been aware of the indictment?" Kobs asked the bishops.

"It's been several months now since we were called to testify," Bishop Barieno replied.

"Go on," Kobs said to Hayes.

"As I said, the issue seems to be the manner in which sexual predators were handled."

"By handled, you mean kept on after the bishops learned of their conduct?"

"That seems likely to be the allegation — that is, if the grand jury issues a true bill — that's an endorsement of the indictment," he said to the bishops.

"Who's been advising these men?" He nodded toward the bishops.

"I have, to this point," Cliff answered.

"And Bill Goulding is the one who presented the indictment to the grand jury?"

"Yes."

Kobs bent his head in thought, then turned to the bishops. "Gentlemen, Bill Goulding is the most competent prosecutor I've ever been up against. He always has his act together. If the grand jury indicts you, trust me, Goulding believes his evidence will convict you twice over. You will need competent legal counsel."

"Where do we go from here?" Bishop Courteer asked.

"The first step is for you gentlemen to decide on your legal counsel. If you decide to choose me, we should understand each other. I will be in charge. I will dictate the defense strategy. You will follow my lead. I will consult with you if the facts require a change in strategy. As for your part, you can fire me at any time. Now, if Goulding has you in his sights, I'd advise you to decide on counsel as quickly as you can. You should have done that when you were first notified of the indictment. Cliff?"

"I suggested that to the bishops at that time. However, in their judgment the matter was too trivial. They felt the investigation would be compelled to exonerate them."

"I see. Well, gentlemen, attorneys Marcie and David will fill you in on our financial requirements. Good day to you all." Kobs rose and walked out of the room.

"Wow," Marcie said when she and David met with Kobs in his office. "We've never seen you like this. You clobbered them. When did you morph from Mr. Congeniality to the Iceman?"

"They needed it, Marcie."

"Why?" David asked.

"Because if they don't understand their limits up front, they will try to micromanage the trial from the outset."

"You're not serious."

"Dead serious. I've dealt with bishops before. They don't know where infallibility stops. They habitually assume their most inane prattle falls under that umbrella. You heard Cliff say these guys considered the matter *trivial*? Rape and sodomy are trivial? What kind of world do these guys live in?"

"You think they'll be back?" asked Marcie.

Kobs shrugged. "Don't know, don't really care. If they come back, they know the terms. Do you think they'll be back, Marcie?"

Remembering two break-ins and one broken side mirror, Kobs parked his Lincoln across the street from the shelter so that it was visible through the storefront windows. He locked the vehicle and walked across the street, debris-scattered thanks to the benign neglect of the City of Chicago. Celina Kobs and Jeanne Goulding, hairnets partially reducing their comeliness, were behind the reconditioned cafeteria table. They cheerfully filled trays as the line of shabbily dressed men and women shuffled by.

Celina saw Jim and waved him over. As he pardoned his crossing through the line he accidentally jostled an elderly man. The man's tray fell to the floor spilling beans, bread, and beef. "My fault," Kobs said. "I'm sorry. You get another tray and come through the line again. I'll clean this up." He led the man to the stack of trays and placed him in the line at that point. Using the spilled tray as a dust pan, he swept the spilled food into it with a couple of paper napkins. Celina tossed him a wet rag and he finished the clean-up. Coming up beside his wife he nuzzled her cheek with his beard.

"You're eating here tonight," Celina said, pressing her cheek close. "That is, if you want a hot meal."

"That's okay. What's up?"

"Ben's here. He'll tell you about it."

He went to the end of the line, unobtrusively stuck a twenty dollar bill in the slot of a coffee can labeled VOLUNTARY CONTRIBUTIONS, and engaged the lady in front of him in conversation.

Jeanne Goulding placed a hunk of roast chuck on his plate with a "Hi Jim. Welcome to Maxim's. Merlot or coffee?"

"Do you have both?"

"No."

"Well, make it coffee then. How's that husband of yours? Celina and I were saying it's been too long since we got together. A month? We should go someplace where they do serve merlot."

"We'd love to. But I've hardly seen him in the last several weeks. He's got a grand jury going."

"Oh? Must be important."

"Jim, I've never seen him so grim. Whatever it is has a total hold on him."

"Ahem," from a voice in the line.

"Oops, I'm holding up the line." He turned to the man behind. "Sorry."

Kobs spotted Ben Bauer's sandy hair and walked toward Ben's table. As he approached, two men seated with Ben picked up their trays and left the table. Kobs took a seat across from Ben. "Hi," he said. God, if all clergy could be like this man, he thought. Straight-arrow tough.

"Jim." Ben smiled and reached a hand across the table.

"Money?"

"How'd you guess?"

The shelter constantly ran on the edge of insolvency. No charitable institution supported it, and the men and women who did support it, with money and volunteer service, were determined to keep it that way. They felt that services to the poor under church or civic sponsorship were often underfunded, overregulated, and used as photo ops by aspiring politicians or posturing prelates.

"How much, Ben?"

"We've got enough for four more days."

"Celina will bring a check tomorrow, enough for two more weeks. That'll give me time to get the word out to our friends, plus muscle a few buddies."

"Thanks."

"My privilege. How are you doing otherwise?

"Good. I love my parish, but my heart keeps coming back here."

Kobs studied Ben's face. Average looks. Not handsome. Not ugly. Pleasant, that's it he thought. Pleasant with a ready smile. "You know, Ben, you don't fit the mold of a Roman-trained guy."

"I hope that's a compliment. Thank God for this place. It helps me keep my head on straight."

"You won't make bishop in this place."

Ben laughed. "I hope to God you're right about that."

Kobs sat at his desk, his broad forehead visible above a newspaper, his feet propped to the side on an open bottom desk drawer. Marcie and David sat at the conference table. They also had copies of the *Daily Sentinel* spread before them. The headlines blared: GRAND JURY INDICTS BISHOPS. They scanned the story:

> With the promises of their Dallas policy of zero tolerance still ringing in the public ear, three bishops are charged with conspiracy under the federal RICO Act, crafted originally to fight the Mafia. Allegedly these three have continued to transfer priests known to them as pedophiles from parish to parish within their respective dioceses. Additionally, they will be charged with conspiracy to accept from and transfer

interstate to each other's jurisdictions priest pedophiles in order to keep them from prosecution.
They will also be charged with jointly conspiring to
covertly aid pedophiles for whom arrest warrants had
been issued, and of which they were aware, to attempt
to flee the country.

U.S. Attorney William Goulding refused to spec-
ulate on the number of sexually abused minors that
might have been spared if these bishops had not been
complicit in the protection of the abusers.

The article went on to identify the bishops as Wilbur Sandes,
bishop of Colchester, NH; Vincent Barieno of Palm Sands, FL; and
Robert Courteer, San Miguel, TX.

It is expected that these bishops will be taken into
custody at about the time this newspaper comes off
the press. If so, they will be flown immediately to
Chicago for a bail hearing. Goulding said he would
oppose bail on the basis of their alleged attempt to
help abusers avoid prosecution by flight to foreign
lands. He feels they might flee to the Vatican.

A spokesperson for the bishops, Monsignor John
O'Malley, decried the grand jury's action as "just another attack from the godless, secularist agenda. These
good bishops will be completely exonerated," he pre-
dicted. He indicated further that the bishops were still
deciding whether to act as their own legal counsel or
seek the service of a defense attorney. "The matter is
so ridiculous and trivial, they're not sure such services
are required," he said.

"If they go without counsel, they're hamburger," Marcie muttered.

"Have you heard anything from Cliff Hayes?" David asked.

At that moment, the phone rang and Kobs picked it up. "Jim Kobs. Oh, hello Cliff. I see your good bishops may take this trivial and ridiculous matter into their own hands. Oh, they have decided. Do they understand the terms?" He listened for several minutes. "Okay. You meet their flights. I'll talk to Bill Goulding on the bail issue. You said the hearing is scheduled for four p.m.? Do you know who the magistrate is? Really, Judge Mildred Monroe? That's interesting. Anyway, I'll meet you and the bishops at the Federal Building at three thirty. That'll give me time enough to explain procedures to them."

"Are we on?" Marcie asked, her eyes sparkling.

"We are. According to Cliff, the bishops' trousers may be dampening."

Chapter Two

The massive stone exterior of the Federal Building with its granite porticoes belied its drab and worn interior. The offices of the U.S. attorney were brightened only by the Department of Justice seal on the door and the U.S. flag in the foyer.

Assistant U.S. Attorney William Goulding sat at his time-worn and scratched desk in a solid oak swivel chair softened by a tired cloth cushion he had purchased at Kmart. Faded dark green file cabinets lined one entire wall of his fourteen-by-fourteen-foot space. Goulding, cropped hair graying at the temples, movie-idol features, and ready smile gave the room its single sparkle. Across the desk from Goulding, FBI agent Kurt Miller absorbed little comfort from a similar cloth cushion on a wooden captain's chair. Except for his alert brown eyes, Kurt's pleasant features and average build made him the perfect invisible-in-a-crowd sleuth. His gaze was fixed on Goulding.

"You did a hell of a job, Kurt," Goulding told him. "I don't remember a more solid string of evidence."

"We had a lot of help," Kurt responded. "Cooperation everywhere. We were in sync with the police departments in all three cities." He studied Goulding. "Is there still a problem?"

Goulding sat pensively for a time, his thumb rubbed back and forth across an eyebrow. "There is one thing I don't understand yet. Even after their Dallas promises of zero tolerance, even after the horrible notoriety of Boston, these bishops kept transferring pedophiles from parish to parish, and from diocese to diocese. They continued to play hardball with the victims."

"They failed to even meet with victims," Kurt interjected. "And they've tied treatment for victims to immunity from legal responsibility, and limited it to their own treatment facilities and personnel."

"They searched for any scapegoats they could dream up rather than assume responsibility," Goulding added. "First they tried to spin eight-year-old victims into seducers, then it was the homosexuals, always it was the media and the secular agenda." He paused.

Kurt took up the list. "Don't forget their failure to report to appropriate civil authorities as the law requires and their failure to notify schools and congregations that they had loosed pedophiles among the children. And don't forget they willfully destroyed files."

"That's enough," Goulding said. "The list drags on. I want to know why. We've got the goods on them. They did all of it. But why? My God what could possibly motivate these guys to put the liberty of sexual abusers above the safety of kids? I'm confident I don't need a clear motive to get a conviction here, but I'd feel more secure if we could nail down the why of it."

"Fear of scandal, damage to the institution? That was inferred last go-around."

"I suspect it's a factor, but hell, that institution has survived scandals of equal or greater magnitude. Think of the Inquisition, the crusades, the torture and murder of dissidents. What's more, they've just been through this same scandal. Why would they risk a repeat?"

"How about money?"

"How money?"

"To protect the church's patrimony."

Goulding's thumb worked his eyebrow. "Again, that might be a part of it. But look at what happened over the past few years. Collections dropped for a while, then quickly rebounded to new highs.

Our good Catholic laity can't seem to face the fact, or they somehow suppress the memory, that Father's touching of their children wasn't an innocent or unintentional gesture. It was rape or fellatio or sodomy or you name it. Their bishops were protecting rapists and sodomites and not the children."

Kurt excused himself. "I've got to make a pit stop."

The phone rang as Kurt left the office. Goulding picked it up. "Bill Goulding."

"Jim Kobs here, Bill. You've been busy."

"Hi Jim. Yes, it's been a rush here. Jeanne tells me she and Celina are going to get us together. It's been a long time."

"Well, I've just been employed by several bishops, so I'll look forward to that dinner, per our custom, when this case is resolved."

"Oh God, I have to put up with your antics through the trial?"

"Enjoy it, Bill. We don't get this opportunity very often."

Goulding laughed. "You're a friend, Jim, but as an opponent at trial, I'd rather face a pack of pit bulls."

"I'm too old for the old pit-bull technique. Bail hearing at four today. What's fair?"

"I'm going to oppose bail, Jim. These guys would be welcome in the Vatican. No extradition agreement there."

"Now who's the pit bull? How about a hundred grand each? That should keep them home."

"It's not their money. Easy come, easy go. They'd leave it on the table in a heartbeat. You know that."

"How much then?"

"The government doesn't print enough."

"Come on, Bill, there are other ways to keep these guys corralled besides jail."

"I'd accept nailing them to a church door."

"Whew, you're tough. I hope the judge is a kinder, gentler —"

"The judge is Mildred Monroe. At least she's the one who authorized the grand jury and will be at the bail hearing."

"Cliff Hayes told me that Millie was the one involved so far. And you think she'll be the trial judge? Manacles Millie? Plank-walk Millie? Hang-em-by-the-toes Millie? Ouch. As if you're not problem enough."

Goulding felt a moment of satisfaction. Mildred Monroe was known as a tough judge when it came to sentencing. But she was a thoroughly fair and competent judge. Know what you're doing in front of Millie, and things worked for you. She punished attorney incompetence severely. Not that Kobs had a problem there. But she wouldn't tolerate obfuscation for obfuscation's sake. Goulding noticed Kurt back at his door. "I've got someone coming in, Jim. I'll see you and your clients at four. Good talking to you."

Goulding waited until Kurt took his seat, then started, "Just look at the nasty characters these bishops protected. The guy who seduced and raped teen-age postulants during their convent training, the guys who sodomized altar boys, Boy Scouts — any boys they could get their hands on — the guys who raped little eight-, nine-, ten-year old girls in their own homes, in the rectory, in the confessional, wherever. And for each of those guys, one or more of these bishops had foreknowledge that these abuses were being perpetrated by each of these priests. They knew about it and didn't do a damn thing. Why? What motive was in their minds before Boston, before Dallas, that's still there? Why no apology except a grudging tsk, tsk out of them? Why do those bishops, totally lacking in sympathy for these crimes or the victims, keep getting the promotions? The *what* we missed the first time around is the *why*, the motive. Sorry, Kurt, didn't mean to give a speech."

"No, don't be sorry. You're making a good point. I don't know the answer, so why don't I go back to the beginning on this?"

"What do you mean, beginning?"

"Check these three bishops out as far back as we can take it. You know, back to their youth. Were they friends? Did they do their training together? How well did they know each other before all this? Were any of them ever alleged to be sexual abusers? Were they part of a clique of abusers? If so, might that clique reach to all these guys they protected and beyond? Could they have been blackmailed by former lovers? That sort of thing."

"You think you can do all that?"

"We can try. The police departments in San Miguel, Palm Sands, and Colchester have been vigorously involved so far. I'm sure we can count on them. And all these guys came from this archdiocese. The Chicago PD here will help all they can. It's a start. If we get something, well, we can go from there."

A small group of people huddled informally around the bench in courtroom 109. The honorable Mildred Monroe's spindly body was fleshed out by the billow of her judicial robes as she tapped the eraser end of a pencil on the bench. She listened to U.S. Assistant Attorney Bill Goulding recommend the retention of the defendants in U.S. custody. When he had concluded she turned to Jim Kobs.

"Mr. Kobs?"

"Your Honor, Mr. Goulding argues for the continued custody of these bishops based solely on his suspicion that they *may* take flight to avoid prosecution." He looked intently into the judge's piercing dark eyes, set narrowly in her thin face. "My reply is simple. These men have no criminal record. They should not be treated as felons until, if, and when they are convicted of a felony. Certainly not on the basis of a prosecutor's slim hunch."

"The charges are for felonies, Mr. Kobs." the judge responded. "And they are charged, among other charges, with abetting the attempted flight of a pedophile. Why would they treat themselves differently?"

"A charge is far from a conviction, Your Honor. The embarrassment of appearing here in handcuffs is itself undeserved. And where would they flee to? They're not charged with being pedophiles so they wouldn't flee to refuge countries in Asia or Africa. Mr. Goulding thinks they might flee to the Vatican. Any flight would be a near admission of guilt. Why would they practically admit guilt and expect the Vatican to welcome them and suffer that embarrassment before the world community? I don't think the Vatican would welcome either them or the subsequent damage to their moral authority."

Monroe studied the bishops, then Goulding, then Kobs. "Bail is set at five hundred thousand dollars each," she said. "The defendants will surrender their passports. Additionally, they will be kept under constant electronic surveillance. Their travel is limited to the confines of their respective cathedral cities and to and from this city for attorney conferences and trial dates. Mr. Goulding and Mr. Kobs, if you will meet me in my chambers please. We can set a date for arraignment while these gentlemen are fitted with tracking devices."

"We'd much appreciate expediting this matter," Bishop Sandes said to no one in particular. "We must get back to substantive matters."

Goulding, who had been placing files in his briefcase, looked at the man incredulously. "When you've forsaken basic justice, sir, what's left for you to be substantive about?"

On his way home after the bail hearing, Goulding dialed the shelter on his cell phone. Jeanne answered.

"Remember me?" he asked."

"Not sure. Are you the window salesman?

"Close."

"You sound familiar. Salesman: used car, driveway sealing, travel agent?"

"All wrong. I'm your husband."

"You're my husband, what's-his-name?"

"Right. I'm Bill."

"Well, hi Bill. Are you in the United States?"

"I'm in the car, a mile from home. When do you get off work?"

"In about an hour."

"Good. How about three days in Door County?"

"Oh, for a minute I thought you really were my husband."

"I'm serious."

"Seriously serious?"

"Absolutely."

"When?"

"We leave first thing in the morning."

"Sounds romantic. Three whole days?"

"Cross my heart. Romantic starts as soon as you get home."

"You are a smoothie. I'll tell Celina she and Ben will be running this place for a few days."

Chapter Three

The arraignment was over. The charges against the three bishops detailed their protective activities given to seven specific priest pedophiles. The pedophiles had eventually all either been convicted in a court of law or had pleaded guilty. All were currently serving prison sentences. Two had been priests under Bishop Sandes, three under Barieno, and two under Courteer.

The charges specified conspiracy on the part of the bishops to protect these pedophiles from the justice system. Their protective activities included: failure to report the sexual abuse activity to proper authorities; payoff of victims with the condition of silence; intimidation of witnesses; transfer of the priest pedophiles from parish to parish and from one of their jurisdictions to that of another; hiding the pedophiles in treatment facilities run by ecclesiastical authority; and, in one instance, an overt attempt to arrange the flight of a charged pedophile to Africa.

The bishops individually entered pleas of not guilty.

Defense attorney Kobs entered motions for dismissal, reduction of bail, and for discovery, the process whereby the prosecution provides the evidence for their charges to the defense. Judge Monroe rejected any reduction of bail, approved discovery, and scheduled a preliminary hearing for November 6, two weeks hence, at which time she would rule on the motion for dismissal. She also set a tentative trial date of May 1.

The war room measured twenty by thirty feet. At one end, sixteen feet of floor-to-ceiling open file shelves, each shelf coursing four feet into the room, ran on tracks across the twenty-foot distance. In front of them, ten more feet of similar shelves also ran on tracks. A self-contained trial preparation area for major litigation cases, the room held a speed copier, computers, sophisticated film and photo equipment, and large areas of table space.

Kobs stood inside the door as dozens of business boxes were wheeled in and stacked along the walls. His motion for discovery had been routine. He knew that Goulding would hold nothing back. This was the stuff of the prosecution's case against the bishops. He walked along one row of boxes reading labels and finding Goulding's meticulous mind reflected there. Bill is depending on straightforward, overpowering evidence, he thought. I'm sure it's all here, but we still have to go through it all. If there's a weak spot we have to catch it.

Back in his office Kobs gave instructions to Marcie and David. "We have six months to go through all that stuff and prepare a defense strategy," he began. "When you read through the trial materials and the guilty pleas of the seven convicted pedophiles, look for any egregious defense attorney lapses. If you don't find any, we are not going to go there during the trial. It will not help our case to spotlight details of the sexual abuse. Goulding will do more of that than we care for. Also, we're not going to revictimize children by making them relive their tragedy."

Kobs sat back in his chair, thumb and forefinger stroking his red stubble beard. "We can be certain that one or more of these bishops were deposed in each of those seven cases. Take care to retrieve any and all indications of their foreknowledge that these men were active pedophiles. Note the timeline from this foreknowledge to the abuse for which those seven were convicted or pled guilty. We want to know every particular in that regard, every source of evidence that they actually had foreknowledge. Then note all evidence of conspiracy on their part. I'm sorry. This conversation is needless. You both know what to look for. When we've got it all together, we'll meet with the bishops to go over our defense strategy. We three will meet every morning at eight to review the findings. Any questions? Marcie?"

Marcie shook her head.

"David?" He looked at the unbalanced features of David's face.

"None."

"Good. Oh, and I won't be in there with you, at least for a while. But I will be on the case — in case you're wondering."

"You know something we don't know?" Marcie asked.

"Not yet. When I do, you'll be the first to know."

Kobs carried a tray through the shelter food line, staffed this night by Celina and two other volunteers. With his tray full, he walked toward Ben Bauer's table, then noticed that another man had Ben's attention. Not wanting to disturb what might be a private conversation, he stopped at another table.

Ben called out, "Hey Jim, there's room here."

"Hi Ben." He recognized the other man as he took a seat across from the two. "How's it going, Chris?" Kobs took in the prematurely creased and shrunken face.

"You wouldn't believe how good it's going, Jim. I've got a lead on a case that will put me back on top. And I'm the frontrunner to get the job."

"Good luck." Kobs had heard it all before. He recalled a youthful Chris, a good lawyer with promise until the promise in a bottle took over. Now the man's practice was all but limited to doing simple wills and collection work for barkeeps to cover his own bills. "What's the case about?"

"It's a dream. Industrial accident. Multiple plaintiffs, close to forty of them. There's millions in it. I've been in touch with most of the victims."

Kobs stared directly into the man's weary dark eyes. "You beat the bottle yet, Chris?"

"Nothing to beat, Jim. You know that. All that about me drinking too much was hooey."

"Seems like I'm getting a whiff of hooey way over here. Don't you think you have to stop?"

"If I had a problem, I'd stop. No problem! Good to see you. I'd better get back on the case. Been burning the midnight oil on this one. Ben. Jim." He nodded at each man and walked away.

"Take care, Chris," Ben called after him.

"You want to take a bet, Ben?" Kobs asked. "On whether that midnight oil is distilled?"

"No bet."

"I know that you work a lot with addicts, Ben. What happens inside their brains?"

"The work I do with them is only to steer them to professionals. I know a little, but I'm no expert. Chris says he doesn't have a problem. Denial is the prime defense mechanism for an addict. The most important thing in Chris's life is his particular fix. Booze. He protects that fix with the ferocity of a mother bear protecting her cubs and with the cleverness of mixed-up thinking."

"The what?"

"AA calls it 'stinkin thinkin'. It protects his fix. He's okay. His career is okay. So there can't be a problem with drinking."

"He's married, isn't he?"

"Was married. When his wife finally saw that she was a partner in his addiction, she got help and said good-bye to Chris. She was fed up with the lies and promises."

"Lies? That really puts it in a morality context."

"Sure, lies. Morally, addicts go downhill faster than boulders off a cliff. They lie to themselves. They lie to everyone else. The fix becomes their moral beacon. If they keep their eyes on that, anything goes. They will lie, steal, and worse to serve the fix. In the world they have created for themselves, basic moral laws don't apply to them. They're special, dispensed from the moral norms the rest of us try to keep. There, we've reached the end of my nonexpertise."

"What I hear you saying is that addiction traps a person in a world of their own."

"That's exactly what happens."

"Did Chris ever get help?"

"Once. I convinced him he needed help. It didn't last. He saw Dr. Georg Hinger a few times and attended a couple AA meetings. The fix was too strong. He simply declared himself cured and, most probably, headed for the nearest bar. If you're interested in more on addiction, I'd recommend Dr. Hinger."

"Tell me about him."

"He's a psychiatrist. An expert on addiction with a national reputation. Lectures at the university here and takes private patients." Ben looked at Jim, who seemed suddenly withdrawn. "You okay?"

"Oh, I'm fine. Just thinking. Ben, it's in the press so you may know I'm representing those three bishops charged with conspiracy in sexual abuse of minors. When I represent anyone I always search for ways to defend them should the prosecution have powerful circumstantial evidence. Frankly, I was puzzled by the behavior of bishops when the scandal first exploded in Boston. It was obvious to me that they had protected pedophiles. Do you agree?"

"That's for sure."

"Why? I keep running possible answers through my brain. The bishops never answered that question. Universally, they just denied any responsibility, or they dissembled. When you mentioned denial in addicts, you made me curious to find if there's any connection. Can you put me in touch with Dr. Hinger?

"Sure."

"Thanks. Did you know any of these three bishops?"

"Not personally," Ben replied. "They were top-drawer guys in the chancery when I was ordained. I met them, but can't say I knew them."

Kobs, Marcie, and David were having their morning conference. The two associates wore clouded looks.

"We've been plowing through the discovery material for four months now," David said. We've gone through about eighty percent of the material. It just keeps getting blacker and blacker. Marcie and I have deposed most of the witnesses the prosecution intends to use. They're solid, solid for the prosecution, that is."

"You knew that all the time, didn't you?" Marcie said to Kobs.

"I didn't know it from the evidence, Marcie. I hadn't looked at that as you know. But I do know Bill Goulding. He's not going to take shots at an institution as powerful as the Catholic Church without having an overabundance of ammo and an overwhelming advantage. Give Goulding a lot of credit. He's got the guts to go after them. I sometimes wonder how this is sitting with the politicians in Washington, who concede considerable electoral power to the bishops in this country. I suspect they're wondering how this case ever got this far, and if they can still stop it."

"Where would Judge Monroe stand on that?" David asked

"Goulding doesn't have to worry about Millie's end. She'd play it fair no matter who the hell the defendant is. No politician is going to influence her."

"Would you want it to end that way?" David asked.

"No. Absolutely not. Bill's a straight arrow. I don't want to see him cut down from behind."

"You'd rather do it, right?" Marcie said.

"Ah, Marcie." Kobs smiled. "You know me too well. We want to win, of course. We owe it to our clients. But we want to win with a fair fight."

Marcie persisted. "How are you going to do that if the evidence keeps piling up against us?"

"Trust me, the evidence will keep piling up."

"Then how?"

"Your discovery work will not be wasted, whatever our strategy turns out to be. It will either show us a weakness in the prosecution's case or —"

"You said it wouldn't show that. Then what?"

"Why, Marcie, then we punt."

"Sometimes you drive me crazy," she replied.

"I won't touch that, Marcie. Then what? Then we use your discovery to convict the bishops before Goulding does."

"Convict them?"

"Right. Convict them in their own minds. Get through to them that they will lose. They will go to prison. That may be the most difficult task of this entire trial."

"Have them plead guilty, or nolo contendere?" David asked.

"No."

"Plea bargain?"

"We might try that, but Goulding won't buy in if you're right about the evidence."

"What then?" Marcie insisted.

"We punt."

"You're driving me crazy, you know that!" Marcie exclaimed.

"I'm following a trail that might lead to crazy, Marcie. Here's where I'm at —"

Chapter Four

The press and television hype brought a crowd to the trial. There was a waiting line when the courtroom door was opened, and the spectator seats filled quickly. Kobs, Marcie, David, and the three defendants were at the defense table fifteen minutes early. Goulding and his assistants were at their table as well. By the time Judge Monroe was announced and proceeded to the bench, the room was full, and people had been turned away.

The courtroom possessed a quiet elegance. The walls were covered with two-by-four foot maple panels varnished to a high shine. The same motif went to the judge's bench, witness stand, and jury box. Maple pews provided seating for approximately ninety-six spectators.

DEENAH

Why do men always look at me? I can feel their eyes going all over me. Just keep your eyes down, Deenah, and keep walking. There's an aisle seat near the front. I'll take that. Maybe this creepy feeling comes from being in a courtroom. It all seems so somber. Okay, sit down and keep from meeting guys' eyes. Why did I come here? Can watching this trial help me? Can anyone help me?

That railing must be what they call "the bar." And I'll bet those men on the left with Roman collars must be the bishops. Just look at that big man with the red hair and trimmed red beard. He must be their attorney. He looks plenty smart. What was his name? Kobs, I think the newspaper said. Those two young people must be his assistants. She's pretty. He looks nice, even if his eyes, ears, nose, and mouth all seem a little off kilter.

I don't want to be here. My therapist advised me to come. She thinks that hearing this trial and facing the issues will help me. Oh, Daddy, when I told you, you wouldn't believe me. Why didn't you believe me? Why didn't you help me?

"I know the man," you said. "He would never do a thing like that. You go to confession and tell God you're sorry. And don't you ever tell me anything like that again. You'll get the whipping of your life." Was it because he was your friend, a priest you could get drunk with?

And Mama, when I told you, you said to just forget it. "Sometimes men do cruel things," you said. "That's the way men are." You didn't help me. How can I forget it?

Get off it, Deenah! No more Daddy and Mommy talk. You're an adult now. What did the therapist call that? Regression?

That man standing directly in front of me must be Goulding. Isn't he handsome? I love that short-cropped hair. Oh, he's looking this way. His eyes are blue. I wonder who the others are. Maybe assistants? Why do I always run from men? Every time one comes close, I freeze up or I run. They tell me that I'm beautiful. I don't feel beautiful.

Why do I keep remembering it all? My therapist says it's because I keep trying to force the images out of my mind. That only makes them stronger. Just let them come, she says. Don't let them alarm you. An image can't hurt you.

He was our pastor, Father Bruce. To all of us kids he was God. He always acted gruff, like we imagined God to be. I can see him in the rectory doorway watching me skip rope on the sidewalk. He crooked a finger for me to come.

"Come into the office, Deenah." His voice was gruff.

I can remember the crucifix on the wall, a golf trophy, and a pic-ture of the pope on his desk. The office smelled smoky.

"Young lady, it's my job as your pastor to teach you secret things. You know what a secret is?"

"Yes."

"Yes what?"

"Yes, Father."

"What we say and do here is a secret. You know what the seal of confession is, don't you?"

"Uh-huh, I mean, yes, Father."

"We'd go to hell if we told anybody our secrets, wouldn't we?"

I was getting scared. "Yeah, I mean yes, Father."

"Promise?"

"I promise."

"Okay, here's a hug."

It seemed like his big belly could drop on my head as I stood there in front of him. My head was at his belt level. Then he un-zipped his pants.

"Pretend it's hard candy," he said.

I turned away, but he grabbed my shoulders and turned me back toward him.

"It's okay. You have to learn." He was gruff again.

I was afraid to refuse. "Always obey the priest," my parents kept telling me. It was awful. He smelled bad, like urine. My stomach churned. How many times did he call me out of the classroom or from the playground to perform that act? I was only nine years old when he first made me do it. And he did it so many times over two years. Why didn't Daddy believe me? Why didn't Mama make it stop? Why didn't these bishops make it stop? Is it too late? Can any-one help me?

JACOB

You're getting old, Jacob. Did you see in the mirror this morning how sparse your gray hair is getting? Did you see how deep the crags are getting in your face? You're seventy-four years old for God's sake. Why are you here? It all happened over sixty-five years ago. You're probably here for some sort of relief. You never told anybody except Mom and Dad, not even Inez. She can't understand why you came to this trial. "Something to do," you told her. Holding poison in causes a bloat. You know that from experience. And it's still in you. When you couldn't hold it anymore you let some of it ooze out in the tears you shed in some private corner.

That pretty young girl next to you can't look at anybody. She's probably afraid. You know what that's like. You were afraid to tell anyone, afraid that they might forever eye you suspiciously, branding you as defective. You did it your way, and you made it. But it still hurts, doesn't it? All kinds of victims have talked. What holds you back? But then, what good would it do after all these decades?

Your heart is beating too fast, Jacob. Think of something pleasant. Remember the farm. See if you can smell the fresh black dirt. Take your time. How about sweet newly cut alfalfa? The warm-sour smells of the barn? Yes. Now try the odor of fallen apples in the orchard? Can you feel the softness of corn silk between your fingers? Yes. The chicken down as you gathered eggs from under the roosting hens? The cold noses of calves searching for milk? Good. Now see if you can still hear the morning crows of roosters in the yard. How about Rex's barking when he frolicked in the pastures? Now pick out all the details of the farm as you look from atop the windmill on the back-forty hill.

There, I feel calm again. I can picture Mom and Dad. They loved us boys like crazy. There's Mom tucking me in bed with a hug and kiss. There's Dad shooting hoops with us boys after our chores. We always liked it when Dad led the rosary. He was the best. He'd whip through it like a jet, blending words and phrases to a mumble.

I might as well repeat the other memory. Sometimes Father Al would lead the prayers. He was slow. He came to the farm a lot in the early afternoons and helped Dad with field work and milking. After supper he'd help Mom with the dishes while Dad cleaned up in the milk house. Then Ma would bathe sister Barbara in the downstairs bathroom while Father Al bathed us boys upstairs.

I was only five, the youngest boy. I was first in line to bathe. I was so innocent. If I ever adverted to the extra time he spent soaping my genitals and buttocks I can't remember thinking it wrong or out of place. He made a game of it. My innocence died when I was seven. It was after a baseball game. He — No, that's enough of that memory. Keep your heartbeat down, Jacob. You know what the doctor said.

JACKSON

Jumping Jesus! Doomsday for the devil I call it. That must be Goulding up there. Smooth, slick-looking devil if I ever seen one. Thinks he can prosecute the Church, does he?

You're in for a surprise, fella. You even look like the devil with those spiked eyebrows. The gates of hell will not knock down my Church, Jesus says. So, smart guy Goulding, guess who you're up against? God versus Goulding. Cripes, I'd like to put some money on this match.

No time off for a trial, the boss tells me. You can shove the job, I says. Jumping Jesus, was he surprised. Thought he was gonna crap in his pants. I wouldn't miss this baby for all the jobs out there. Hey, this place is filling up fast.

I'm sold on those numbers. It's scientific. God made the world using numbers. I figure if you can put all the right numbers together you'd be the smartest guy in the world. And man, weren't those numbers something last night. Lucifer and two devils come out at 180. Two Gouldings come out at 180. You can't tell me that's a coincidence. Those things just don't happen. I was telling the wife about it. Look, I says to her, "it's simple. *A* equals one, *Z* equals twenty-six." You're Lucy. I had my numbers chart there. Lucy is twelve plus twenty-one plus three plus twenty-five. You're a sixty-one. Compare that to other words you want to check out. You'll be surprised what you come up with. It goes back to some Greek guy named Pitheegorus, or something like that. If he did it in Greek, I figure I can do it in English numbers. It's my own system, and I've come up with some great stuff, let me tell you. Someday I'm gonna write a book on it. Pop always said I was the smartest of the litter. "Yore like a submarine," he'd say. "Yore thinkin' runs deep." Lucy says she thinks it's a bunch of crap. What can you expect of a dumb broad? No wonder God wants guys to run things.

I figure I ain't never been closer to God than I am here, not even in church. Figure it out, Jackson, I says to myself. Three bishops on trial and God ain't going to be close by? Wouldn't be surprised to see some exciting stuff. Maybe God'll dump the judge's bench on top of Goulding and mash him to a pulp. Now that would be better than a race car pileup any day. Maybe an earthquake, a big explosion. Who knows? Most people are just too dumb to see the possibilities here. Thank God. Jumping Jesus, how would you ever get in here if they all wanted in.

ROELLY

Mary's hand seems cold in mine. She's not crazy about being here. I can't keep my mind on the prosecutor's introductory remarks. All I can think of is you, Barieno, you bastard. At first, I couldn't believe you had abused Paul when you were stationed at St. Sebastian's. We were friends. At least Mary and I thought you were our friend. Now I can barely stand the sight of you. When you turned and looked at us a few minutes ago, you didn't even know us. People and friendship obviously don't mean a damn thing to you. How does an abuser become a bishop? Is that how it is with you guys? You're a pedophile, so you protect pedophiles? Are all of you guys pedophiles?

Someone ought to make you look at Paul's joyless face for the rest of your life. You stole his youth. You planted torture in a boy's head where happiness should be. What can be more important to you bishops than kids' safety? I can't understand you. You're supposed to be our moral leaders, men who have studied what justice is all about. How does keeping predators loose among kids fit in with justice? Can you get more warped than that?

At first we didn't understand what happened to change Paul. Finally, his school counselor got the story out of him and the two of them told Mary and me. We couldn't believe it at first. We had put our complete trust in you, Barieno. I don't like to think I didn't have the balls to confront you then. But I didn't.

We got Paul into therapy. Both Mary and I have decent jobs, but the expenses just got too much for us. The counselor suggested we ask the diocese for assistance. Did that ever stir up a hornet's nest. The cardinal refused to even meet with us and sent us a scorching letter telling us we were defaming "a good, holy priest." Holy, my ass! Next, he sicced his attorneys on us. Since we had no proof of the abuse other than Paul's word, they said it would be his word against that of "a good, holy priest." "If you go to the police or sue," they told us, "we will counter-sue. We will bury you in expenses." How's that for a loving, caring shepherd? Both Mary and I were afraid to confront that army. We retreated and emptied our retirement accounts to keep Paul going. And we'll do what has to be done.

About the time I was ready to take you on face-to-face, you disappeared. The cardinal had transferred you to the chancery office. We were told it was a big promotion. Then a few years after that we hear you'd made bishop. God Almighty!

So what's more important than kids to you? Is being a priest so high and mighty that, even if you're a pedophile, bishops give you protection rather than your victims? Didn't you guys learn anything from Boston? Didn't the *zero tolerance* you promised in your Dallas meeting mean a damn thing? I hope Goulding buries you bastards. He's fighting a fight I should have fought against assholes like Barieno. I can't make any excuses for myself. I should have shot the bastard.

Was that Governor Keating right when he said you bishops are like the mafia? You're worse! I can't see the mafia setting pedophiles loose on the street.

Mary's gripping my hand like there's no tomorrow. We're both old beyond our forty-two years. She's got tears in her eyes. God, that claws at my heart. You bastards all belong in hell.

The courtroom was hushed as Goulding called his first witness to the stand. The witness had been the district attorney who successfully prosecuted the Reverend James T. Borkamp, one of the seven priest sex offenders with whom these three bishops were allegedly coconspirators.

After the witness's biographical detail had been recorded, Goulding asked, "District Attorney Doyle, please give the court a brief summary of the crimes for which Reverend Borkamp was tried and convicted."

"Certainly. The case against Borkamp goes back to when he was the chaplain at a local convent. The nuns call it their motherhouse. It's where girls are trained to be nuns. Among his assigned duties, Borkamp was confessor and spiritual director to the aspirants.

"What exactly are aspirants?"

"Those are young girls who aspire to be nuns but are too young to be accepted as postulants or novices. They're only high school students."

"Your Honor," Kobs broke in. "The defense will stipulate to the conviction or confession of all seven pedophiles. There's no need for this detail, nor is there a need to waste the court's time."

"There is a need, Your Honor," Goulding countered. "This detail goes to show the nature of the crimes for which these bishops are charged as coconspirators."

"Defense request denied," Judge Monroe directed. To the witness, "You may continue, Attorney Doyle."

"Borkamp would give devotional talks to the group of aspirants, at that time a total of seven girls. His favorite theme was to liken the girls to brides, brides of Jesus. He told them how privileged they were to be chosen by Jesus as his brides. Then he would have them lie on their backs and spread their legs. It was, he said, 'a physical expression of their absolute trust in Jesus.' Those innocent, naïve, and idealistic girls readily obeyed him. 'Jesus will impregnate you with all that is holy,' he told them. The girls testified later that they would leave these sessions feeling adult and elated."

"Objection, Your Honor," Kobs interjected. "This kind of detail serves no purpose."

"Overruled. Go on, Attorney Doyle."

"During spiritual direction sessions with them individually, he would lead them through the same routine. It didn't take him long to determine which girls were the most naive of the seven. He would carry the exercise further with three of the girls. 'Imagine Jesus holding you in his arms,' he would say, and then lead each one through a series of romantic scenes for her to imagine. He then told them he would be Jesus to them. He wanted them to experience the ecstasy of loving Jesus. He removed their panties and had sexual intercourse with them. At the end, he would admonish them not to tell anyone.

To tell or describe their experience would be to betray Jesus, their husband, whose intimacy was for them alone. Those young sheltered girls believed him."

"Objection again, Your Honor," Kobs interjected. "This kind of detail serves no purpose."

"Overruled. Please continue, Attorney Doyle."

"His actions only came to light when one of the aspirants became pregnant. The nun director of the aspirants got the real story from each of the seven girls. She reported it to the bishop. The nun testified at the trial that the bishop, Bishop Sandes, imposed silence on her and the girls under holy obedience."

"What do you mean by holy obedience?"

"Basically it means do it because Sandes said so."

"What happened to Borkamp?" Goulding asked.

"Sandes transferred him to another parish."

"What was his behavior there?"

"He soon selected out of the seventh and eighth grades a small group of pious girls and organized them into a devotional sodality he called "Brides of Christ." You can probably guess what happened next. He successfully raped several of those young girls in a school office before a teacher walked in one day and caught him in the act. Evidently, in his eagerness, he had neglected to lock the door. The teacher immediately informed the parents and went with them to the pastor and to the bishop. Bishop Sandes offered them money under the condition of silence. The teacher and the parents then took the matter to the police."

"Is that when you prosecuted him?" Goulding asked.

"Not yet. During the investigation process Borkamp disappeared. We learned later that Bishop Sandes had transferred him to Bishop Courteer's jurisdiction. Sandes sent Courteer a laudatory endorsement of Borkamp, but did not mention the pedophilic behavior. The evaluation was obviously a self-serving piece meant for the file. Investigators found a personal handwritten note from Sandes in Courteer's correspondence files. In the note Sandes told the real story. A secretary had filed that letter contrary to Courteer's direction to destroy it.

"We finally caught up with Borkamp. He had organized another 'Brides of Christ' sodality in the parish to which Courteer assigned him. Our investigators found that he had already raped at least one girl. We brought him back to Colchester, prosecuted, and won a conviction. He is now serving a twenty-five-year sentence in prison."

"Is it a requirement of law in New Hampshire that knowledge of pedophilic activity be reported to the police?"

"Yes, it is. Absolutely," Doyle replied.

"Did Bishop Sandes ever report his knowledge of Borkamp's pedophilic activities?"

"No, he did not. In fact, before Borkamp's trial, when we deposed Bishop Sandes, he denied any foreknowledge, even when confronted with the contradictory witness of the nun director of aspirants, the testimony of the teacher who caught Borkamp in the act, and the letter in his own handwriting to Bishop Courteer. In short, he lied under oath."

"Thank you, District Attorney Doyle." Goulding turned to Kobs. "Your witness."

"No questions," Kobs replied, his eyes on the doodles he was penning on a legal pad.

"Your next witness then, Mr. Goulding," Judge Monroe directed.

"I call Sister Maureen Delaney to the stand," Goulding said.

FABIAN

I'm going to like this assignment. Any reporter my age would like it. When your head is bare and the fringe is gray, when your legs complain at the overlap hiding your belt, and when your mind screams for an espresso jump start to each day, it's nice to sit down on a job for a change.

This trial will take weeks, maybe months. I get to relax in the boredom of it all, maybe even a nap now and then. A few notes during the day, a quick call-in of my summation at five, and I'm free. Then a cocktail, steak dinner, and a comfortable hotel room all on *True Catholic.* I've got every one of Walker Percy's novels in my bag. If Rachel were alive and with me, this would be perfect.

My editor, Ralph, says to write it as I see it. Helen, the owner of *True Catholic,* smells conspiracy. She always smells conspiracy. "It's there," she says to me. "Look for it. See who's behind it." She thinks secular humanists lurk everywhere, those unscrupulous terrorists always at the ready to set off bombs loaded with anti-Catholic shrapnel. Thank God Ralph keeps her at bay.

I don't believe this is a conspiracy. The prosecutor is a Catholic in good standing. I've checked that out. He's just doing his job, a tough job I'd say. It's certainly not a career-building task to confront the Catholic hierarchy with their foibles, if such these are.

Hopefully these bishops will be exonerated. The church has to get this scandal behind it. My guess, preliminary as it is, says they're not guilty of a crime. True, they exhibited concern for the abusers, but we're supposed to bring back the sinner. Isn't that the Christian thing to do? So, go after the abusers, not the bishops who were just being good Catholics. I am distressed by the way bishops appear to have shown little sympathy for the victims. I suppose, like any of us, they can't keep their eyes on everything. And then, when the victims began going after tons of money, well, bishops had to draw a line in the sand somewhere. After all, they bear responsibility for the church's patrimony.

The best scenario: This trial will provide a forum for the Church to hold aloft its eternal truths for the world to see. I just hope it won't give more fodder to the liberals. In my mean moments, I think God turned Satan loose in our times in the shape of liberals. Their questioning of time-tested sexual mores, their acceptance of homosexuality and divorce. I mean, where does inclusion stop? The Church must get this scandal behind it — quickly.

RENEE

Renee removed a small cosmetic mirror from her purse and began a covert examination of her hair and face. She should have taken the time in the apartment, she thought, patting a stray strand of blonde hair into place. She did a quick check of her face. She tucked the mirror back in the purse, sat back in her rear corner seat, and surveyed the courtroom.

She might as well be here as anywhere, she thought, since she had no job to go to. Maybe she'd learn what makes bishops tick. They'd cost her the sweetest job she could imagine. She'd give anything to be back in the classroom again, facing the challenge of young adult minds. She loved those students.

An associate professor, Renee had taught ethics. She returned to the classrooms in her mind. Class by class, she went down the rows of seats, naming the students as she went. She had a special affection for the seminarians who dotted each classroom. Their idealism shone from their eyes and in their papers. In one of her lectures she had presented the ethical and historical foundations for women's full equality. She maintained that equality was ethically achieved only when there were no barriers to careers for which anyone was capable — anyone — including women. She had wondered aloud why that ethical standard didn't presently apply to the priesthood. A few students responded with quizzical looks, but she thought nothing of it. They had never come to her with their questions.

She realized now that some seminarians had reported what she had said to their rector. The rector, in turn, had reported her words to the bishops who sponsored the young men. She was naïve she realized, but as a tenured professor she felt secure. Had the subject of justice come up, she'd been confident that there, in a Catholic institution, fairness would prevail — until she received a summons to the dean's office.

She could still picture the pudgy, stern-faced monk standing behind his desk in the brown Franciscan habit. He looked grim, his eyes cold.

"You have been judged unfit to teach Catholic doctrine," he said. "That being the case, your employment is terminated effective immediately."

Shocked, stunned, she'd demanded to be told the basis of her dismissal. What had she taught that made her unfit? What opportunity would she have to defend herself?

"I have nothing more to say," the dean said, his demeanor unrelenting. "I'm advised by my attorneys not to get into those matters. Good day! May God be merciful to you."

She learned later from faculty friends that the termination of her employment had been demanded by three bishops, whose names she was never given. *Do bishops know how important jobs are to people?* she had wondered. They are secure in their abundance, but can't seem to relate to everyday needs of other people. They preach a social gospel, but they can take jobs away without allowing a defense.

Her friends notified the American Association of University Professors of her peremptory dismissal. In turn, the association accused the university of violating the principle of academic freedom, which it had publicly espoused. Their advocacy went nowhere, and in the often used hierarchical reliance, the passage of time buried her case beneath memory. But not her memory.

So now she looked for a faculty position. Interviews at both Northwestern University and the University of Chicago offered promise.

Bishops had seen no need for justice in her case. Now that some of them stood before this tribunal of justice, she wondered how they felt.

She would be meeting with Ben tonight. The priest exhibited a splendid combination of gentility and intellect. She could not have handled this trauma without his quiet wisdom.

"Your questions are my questions," he had told her. "Let's work through them together."

Chapter Five

SISTER MAUREEN

Get them, Goulding! Those bishops won't learn until they experience humanity from the other side of prison bars. Prison is the only answer. It'll keep their heads out of the clouds. I know Sandes. I've been on the receiving end.

I was happy to be a witness against Borkamp and now against Sandes. The memory of catching Borkamp raping that little girl is as vivid to me as the day it happened. I caught him red-handed, pants down, and in the act. He wasn't even embarrassed, just angry. "How dare you?" he said to me.

Wouldn't you think a teacher would get a "thank you, Sister" for helping put that abuser out of reach of kids? What I got was fired. The pastor called me from school a few days later and fired me. Cold turkey! He accused me of defaming the good name of a priest of God.

I was stunned. Teaching is my life. I love it. I love the children. Sister Betty tried to reconcile the matter with the pastor. He was adamant. Then she complained to Sandes, and he upheld the pastor.

Sandes didn't know our Betty. She wasn't elected president of our congregation because of her pious looks. She has guts. She pulled all the nuns out of that school, half the teaching staff. Then it was the pastor's turn to complain. He went to Sandes again. Sandes ordered Betty to send the nuns back. She refused. We took a vote. Every single one of the sisters supported Betty. It's time for women to shed our unthinking obeisance to those knuckleheads.

I'm praying for you, Goulding. I've searched my soul and I know it's not out of a spirit of revenge. I don't want that. I want to get our Church back on track, and, sad to say, only the bishops stand in the way.

Flanked by the defendant bishops, Kobs watched with admiration as Goulding moved the prosecution forward with practiced logical precision. His questioning of a district attorney from a small New Hampshire town detailed the prosecution of Reverend Carl Stauffurter. As before, Goulding's questioning drew a straight line from the pedophile acts of the priest through discovery of those crimes, through Sandes's foreknowledge of the priest's pedophilic activity, through the bishop's continued exposure of children to the priest, to the bishop's continued denial of foreknowledge.

"What were Stauffurter's seduction methods?" Goulding asked.

"He owned a rather secluded cottage, actually a three-bedroom ranch-style house, on a lake in northern Massachusetts, about an hour's drive from Colchester. On Sundays, after the last Mass, he would pack several boys into his van and drive to the cottage for a one- or two-day stay. The boys ranged in age from nine to twelve. At the lake he would treat the boys to a variety of activities that captured their enthusiasm. In the summer they would fish, sail, water ski, and swim. Swimming was always in the nude. In the fall and spring they would hike, fish, play softball or volleyball. In winter ice sailing, downhill and cross-country skiing were available. In all four seasons, all indoor activities were in the nude.

"At night he would generally have two boys in each bed. They would sleep in the nude. And he always had one boy sleep with him. From the boys' testimony he would, without any seductive talk or action, fellate that boy and follow that with forced rectal copulation."

"How did he keep those activities unknown to the parents?"

"He read boys very well and ensured their silence either through the intimation they would lose all the fun things they enjoyed at the cabin, or through threats of hell and damnation for the boy and his family. He was able to come up with whatever worked."

"How did it all come to light?"

"One of the parents heard a group of boys talking about it. She found out from her son the names of other boys, and then met with their parents. En masse they went to Bishop Sandes. He listened and promised he would investigate the matter and deal with the priest appropriately. A few of the parents, distrustful of the bishop, went to the police who began their own investigation."

"What did Bishop Sandes do?"

"He transferred the priest to a hospital chaplaincy where, or so Sandes promised the parents, the man would have no contact with children."

"And then?

"The bishop didn't alert the nuns who ran the hospital of the priest's proclivities. He said daily Mass at the hospital and, of course, the nuns recruited altar boys to assist."

"Did he take those boys to the cottage and assault them?"

"Yes, within weeks of his reassignment."

"Obviously then, that activity was discovered," Goulding said.

"Yes it was. The father of one of the boys in the earlier group had made it his business to spot-check the priest's cottage from a fishing boat. He saw the renewed activity and nude boys and reported it to the police. The police informed the hospital nuns of prior allegations against Stauffurter and began interviewing the involved boys. The nuns began utilizing adults to assist at Mass. They also reported their suspicions to Bishop Sandes.

"The police interviewed the bishop, who expressed surprise and total ignorance of any allegations against 'this good, caring priest.' At the same time, he sent the priest to a treatment center in Maryland. There, Stauffurter was confirmed as a pedophile and Bishop Sandes was notified. When the priest returned to the diocese a month later, the psychiatrists at the center sent a letter to the bishop to the effect that Stauffurter should be kept out of all ministry. The bishop appointed Stauffurter to another parish. And he continued sexually abusing children.

"At that time, the police brought the results of their investigation to our office. We prosecuted and Stauffurter was convicted."

"Did Bishop Sandes testify at the trial?"

"No. We had deposed him prior to the trial."

"Did he ever explain why he kept transferring Stauffurter to new assignments where he could be expected to prey on young boys?"

"He described all reports to him of Stauffurter's activity as ugly rumors, not accusations. The witnesses at the trial made it clear they had clearly reported the priest's specific pedophilic activity to the bishop."

"In other words, Bishop Sandes knew what was going on long before the trial?"

"Yes."

"He could have stopped that activity?"

"Clearly, yes. He should have stopped it after the first accusations. He had the power to remove Stauffurter from all ministry, and report it to the police."

"He never reported the priest to the authorities?"

"Never."

"Thank you. No further questions."

"Your witness, Mr. Kobs," Judge Monroe said.

Kobs was practicing calligraphy. Without raising his head he responded. "No questions, your honor."

BISHOP SANDES

I forbid my face to register this humiliation. The Lord's words fill and sustain me: "Blessed are you," he said, "when they insult you and persecute you and utter every kind of slander against you because of me. Be glad and rejoice, for your reward is great in heaven; they persecuted the prophets before you in the same way."

All my life I have kept my sights on God. My energies have followed a straight line, blinders on, to proclaim and enhance His glory. If I can boast about anything in my own regard, I can honestly say that much.

When I was ordained to the fulness of the priesthood as a bishop I kept my focus on that one goal. It has not been easy. Command never is. Sometimes it calls for an iron fist. Sometimes people get hurt. Sometimes a leader must shed hatred and scorn like rain from a slicker. I've been through all that.

Sadly, my most difficult obstacle has been the opposition from my own priests, especially from my closest priest advisors. Some memories are painful still.

"Nine hundred thousand to remodel the bishop's residence?" Monsignor Ryan asked at one meeting.

He appeared incredulous as did the other advisors. I knew then my own need for a firm will and the patience to instruct them. "Do you think I'm some sort of missionary bishop?" I asked. "Do you expect a successor of the apostles, the representative of Christ the King in Colchester diocese, to live in a mud hut?"

"The bishop's residence already compares favorably with the better homes in the city," he countered.

"It should be the very best," I insisted.

"How will we pay for it?" another asked.

"The money is already in the bank for the remodeling," I replied.

We will have to raise the money for the new cathedral." I watched their faces as that message struck home.

"Cathedral?" Ryan asked.

"Yes, a cathedral. The one we have is too small, too old, and too ugly. It is completely unworthy. I'm embarrassed to celebrate the liturgy there. And I am confident that the Lord shares my embarrassment."

"It's a charming building," Ryan said. "It has a feeling of hospitality about it. It has a history of warmth and welcoming for our people and priests. Most of our diocesan priests were ordained in its sanctuary."

"It's an embarrassment to God," I insisted. "His honor and glory demand more of us."

"How much?" they asked, almost simultaneously.

"Forty to sixty million. We'll have a closer estimate once the plans are completed. You will each receive a preliminary design from the architects within the month. Once you have studied that, we will meet again to discuss it." I could see they were stunned.

"Where will that kind of money come from?" another asked.

"We are a small diocese," I responded, "but not a poor diocese. There are men and women of wealth here. When I mention knighthood or papal lady status to them, I can read their desire. Passing out a few honors will bring in a sizeable share of the cost. We will borrow the rest and put a tax on the parishes."

"Can't money of that amount be put to better use?" Ryan again.

"What better use than to visibly show the power and glory of God?" I looked around at their sullen faces. I spoke kindly, I think. "Consider the great churches of Rome, Fathers," I said. "Saint Peter's, Saint Mary Major, Saint John Lateran, Saint Paul Outside the Walls. Think of the joy they bring to people from all over the world. Think of the faith they stir in the people who visit them. Think of the honor they bring to the papacy and thereby to God. Think of the magnificence of Chartres Cathedral, the centuries of faithful workers it took to build it, the omnipotence of God it speaks to visitors. We, here in Colchester, share that heritage of faith and that will to give glory to God. We will do our part. We will not be slackers. We will make our contribution to what has been so aptly called 'The Church Visible.'" I looked around again at their now expressionless faces. "And a people of abundant faith will be the byproduct of our efforts."

They grumbled, but the remodeling of my residence is completed, the old cathedral razed, and the new one under construction. I haven't told my priest advisors yet, but the next project will be a shrine, a place of pilgrimage to equal Lourdes in France and Saint Anne de Beaupré in Quebec. God's grandeur will shine forth from those projects long after I'm gone. They will strengthen the faith of generations to come. And I will carry a portfolio of them to my grave. It will be my passport to eternal life. I can hear the voice of God speaking to me: "Well done, good and faithful servant. Enter into your eternal reward."

As for this trial, people don't see the big picture. They don't put this sexual abuse thing into context. It, too, has to do with God's glory because it relates to "The Church Visible." I saw clearly that my visible Church would be scarred by the sins of those priest abusers if it became a public scandal. I did all I could to keep that from happening. And I did all I could for those poor priests who were ordained to be visible signs of a God present to His people. They sinned and failed to measure up. I apologize to no one. I would not do things differently.

Kobs sat across the table from Ben Bauer. The crowd at the shelter had thinned, but there was still a half hour of serving time. Celina and Jeanne were behind the counter, eating their meals as the line permitted.

"Ben," Kobs began, "I've been spending a lot of time at the university talking to professors. Dr. Hinger, but also with anthropologists, historians, and psychologists. I think I'm making some headway there. Tell me what it's like being a priest. That might fill in some blanks."

"Where do you want me to start?"

"How about the beginning, when you were ordained?"

Ben was thoughtful for a moment, his eyes on the past. "Ordination day was a family day. My entire family was there, Mom and Dad, my two brothers and two sisters, and their spouses. I've heard married couples say they can't remember details of their wedding day, who was there, who said what, stuff like that. That's the way my ordination day was. I do remember who was there, just my family. But other than that it's a blur. A wonderful blur, though."

He took a sip of coffee. "The day I remember most was the day I celebrated my first Mass and the reception that followed. The church and the reception hall were crowded. The sermon was given by my dad's brother, a Maryknoll priest. I don't remember what he talked about. What I remember most is the way people treated me, the deference they gave me. People who the day before might have called me shithead, now called me Father. There was a kind of soft awe and reverence in their voices." He sipped more coffee.

Kobs stared into the clear blue of Ben's eyes. "How did you react to all that?"

"If I'm honest, I have to say I ate it up. I was king of the hill. I thought it and I felt it. You going to eat that cookie?" he asked, pointing at the chocolate chip pastry abandoned on Kobs's tray.

Kobs pushed the tray across to Ben.

"Thanks. It goes with my carb diet. The doctor told me to gain five pounds, minimum."

"You're welcome. Back to king of the hill."

"Okay. It took me probably two or three months to come down from that high. I don't know exactly what caused reality to set in. I think it was the people. I saw clearly that if I was a shithead before ordination, I was still a shithead. That insight saved me. It was a greater blessing than my ordination."

"What do you mean by 'saved me'?" Kobs asked.

"I realized that it wasn't about me. It was about the people who displayed that deference. They needed a place, someone, in whom they could deposit trust, someone to whom they could transfer the power that trust bestows. We all need that. It was their need, not me, that they expressed at my reception and continue to express every time they call me *Father*.

Both men were silent, both sipped coffee.

"Jim, it scared the hell out of me."

"What did?"

"The direction their trust almost took me."

"Can you explain that?"

"I can try. Like I said — and I believe this applies to all priests — we begin to see ourselves as special. That was even drilled into us as seminarians. We were told we had a higher calling. Read higher as above the common people. We were told we were God's elite. For some reason that never caught on with me when I was in the seminary. But it did at ordination. Suddenly I was a member of the club, the clerical kingdom. And I was going to do big things for God."

"What sort of big things?"

"When my work with real people woke me up to the real world, I realized that doing big things translated as being somebody, a *noticed* man. That's what scared me. I turned around, faced the real world of real people where little things get the job done."

"Were you ever tempted to turn back?"

"No, but I was scared I might be. That other world has its allure: power, prestige, wealth, privilege—all that. So I set up roadblocks."

"I've a need to play the attorney here," Kobs said. "You used the phrase 'other world.' Explain that."

Ben was thoughtful. "Let's take it in steps." He took another bite of his cookie. "You know that I studied and was ordained in Rome. After I served in a parish for two years, they asked me to go back to Rome and get a degree in canon law. I had been *noticed*. With a Roman background and a degree in canon law I would be destined for a career starting in the chancery office. There I'd get the opportunity to be *noticed* on a regular basis. I know my strengths. I can be an entertaining guy and all that. I can read the politically correct in the clerical context. I can say the right things. I could suck up without the sucking sound being heard."

"Who asked you to go to Rome? The Cardinal?"

"Presumably. I don't know for sure. It came from the chancery."

"What did you do?"

"I turned it down."

"You were allowed to do that? What about your promise of obedience?"

"I told them I wouldn't go under any circumstance."

"And they took it?"

"They need priests. So I got away with it. But he let me know in explicit terms that I had 'burned all bridges.' He meant the bridges to that other world."

"Who's he?"

"In this instance it was the auxiliary bishop in charge of personnel."

"How clear is your picture of the world on the other side of those burned bridges, that other world?"

"Clear enough. I experienced it as a student in Rome, and even at the parish level."

"Example?"

"When I refused to go to Rome, I was assigned to a suburban parish, a very wealthy suburban parish. The pastor there is a monsignor — translate that as *my lord* — who had a sparsely disguised desire to be a bishop. I spent a lot of time instructing people who wanted to be Catholic. The one example that says it all involved a paraplegic. When I baptized him I was summoned by the monsignor and told bluntly that 'we don't want that kind in our parish.' The monsignor's world didn't have a place for visibly disabled people. It was clear to me that God's world has a place for them. They're all around us. I lasted about ten months before the monsignor pulled strings to get me out."

"Okay, but isn't that just an example of one quirky guy? Are you saying that he represents everyone on the other side of the bridge?"

"In a way he does. The other side of the bridge has been described as the 'purple kingdom.'"

"Oops! I see that Celina and Jeanne are ready to leave," Kobs said. "I'd like to continue this conversation. Are you free to come over to the house? Or perhaps you'd give me an appointment."

"I'm free tonight. Let's go," Ben replied, taking the last bite of the cookie.

Driving his Chevy, Ben followed Jim and Celina. The three were in the Kobs's paneled study twenty minutes later.

"What's your poison, Ben?" Kobs asked.

"What are you having?"

"Scotch."

"I've always wanted to try Scotch, just never got around to it. I'll join you."

"Celina?" Kobs asked his wife who had taken her tall and trim body to a seat next to a bright light on the opposite side of the study.

"Nothing now, Jim," she answered, already buried in a book.

Drinks in hand, the two men took chairs at a large bay window that looked out on a small lake. Dusk blurred the images of scurrying ducks. "We were at the purple kingdom," Kobs said.

"And in that kingdom is found a purple culture, e.i.e.i.o," Ben chimed. "Sorry about that, it just came out. Let's go back to the bridge first. The majority of guys wake up like I did, turn away from the bridge, and go down various dusty roads. But there are some who look across and see the lush pastures of purple grass. They pay the toll, cross over, and may never look back. What's ahead of them consumes all their attention."

"The sucking up?"

"Let's just say they feel themselves to be special, and being special to those above them — bishops, archbishops, cardinals, the pope — is soul food. More accurately, it's ego food. These guys are not lazy. They will work like dogs to court *notice* from the person above them. As they advance, the purple gets deeper, richer, and eventually royal. They feel truly special. In the purple culture this monarchical-type hierarchy is decreed to be of divine origin. You can't get more special than that."

"Are you saying that all bishops buy into that?"

"No, not all. Some, I'd guess it's a minority though, can still look back over the bridge and feel genuine kinship for the people there."

"Less than half?"

"It seems that way to me. A few understand that the monarchical imitations, the royal insignia, the purple parts, are self-serving accretions taken on down through the centuries. But most seem to find an appeal in the lordship qualities. For them that culture takes over. They become captives. The accretions become a necessary part of their legitimate authority and perks. And of course, it's God who has legitimized all of it. It becomes for them a trap, a grandiose trap."

"What do you mean by trap?"

"In my opinion, they soak up this grandiosity until it becomes an emotional and mental habit. It is to them the only true culture. It becomes the only one they know, or remember. It's difficult for any of us to understand a foreign culture. We are all trapped in some way in our own culture. The purple culture is no exception." Ben took a sip of Scotch, held it in his mouth, and put the glass down, a motion more like pushing it away.

"Not everybody likes Scotch," Kobs said, catching Ben's facial reaction. "How about something else?"

"Water's good," Ben replied. "How can you drink this stuff?"

"It's an acquired taste. Let's say it has become part of my culture." Kobs left the room and returned with water.

"That stuff is almost as distasteful as the purple culture," Ben teased.

Kobs laughed. "I have no other faults. Ask Celina."

"Ask Celina what?" Celina asked from across the room. "You should know, Ben, that I usually have no trouble tuning Jim out, but not when he uses my name. Then I come to arms."

"He says his only fault is Scotch," Ben said.

"I told him once that good conversation calls for a bit of exaggeration, but he carries it beyond any reasonable limit," Celina answered. "When you've got an afternoon free, I'll give you a list of his faults. Be warned though. It's not entertainment."

"Sorry to disturb you, Celina," Kobs said. He turned to Ben, smiling. "Do you think something in the purple culture allowed so many bishops to put the protection of pedophiles ahead of the children those guys abused?"

"That's a heavy question. It's possible, even likely." Ben said thoughtfully. "As I said, there's privilege, power, prestige, wealth, and the whole bag of princely goodies in the purple culture. Years ago it was theologized that this culture formed the perfect society."

"So, you're saying if the purple men become so grandiose as to think that it's all theirs by right, that it's God-given and God-mandated, and they are in the upper tier of God's buddies, then in their minds they would have the duty to protect it if threatened? Wouldn't that be God's own priority?"

"It's possible. I've just never taken the time to put all the pieces in order. Some people say it's all about power. I think the purple culture is more complex than that. If it's all about power, it's also all about the trappings of power. It's about the culture."

"Thanks, Ben. You've given me something to reflect on, something that may help me in my legal work. I'm grateful. Are you sure I can't replace that water with lemonade or soda or something?"

"I'm fine, Jim."

"Have you been following the trial?"

"A little."

"What do you think?"

"If they're really guilty, they should go to jail like anybody else would."

Kobs pondered Ben's response. "There are worse punishments than jail, Ben."

Chapter Six

Angry eyes protruded from Bishop Sandes. "Why aren't you doing something?" he demanded. "All we hear from you is 'no questions,' 'no questions.' Is that all you can say?"

The three bishops and Kobs, Marcie, and David were meeting at the insistence of the bishops in a conference room at the law firm.

"What would you suggest?" Kobs asked calmly.

"Attack the witnesses!"

"Specifically?"

"That's your job," Sandes exclaimed.

"My job is to keep you out of jail."

"I don't see you doing anything to accomplish that!"

"That's because I'm not doing anything that's visible to you."

"What are you doing?"

"So far," Kobs responded, "it's more a question of what I'm not doing."

"What is that supposed to mean?" Sandes grumbled.

Kobs leaned forward, elbows on the table. "It means, for example, that I'm not attacking witnesses whom we have already deposed and found to be credible and unassailable. It means, for example, that I'm not about to willy-nilly get in the way of the jury hearing the prosecution's case. To do so is to risk resentment by the jury and a questioning of our tactics. We want a jury with open minds when we come to presenting a defense. We want as much goodwill from them as we can get, and there may not be much left."

"But Goulding is killing us!" Sandes slumped back in his chair.

Kobs continued in a comforting voice. "Also, for example, I often will not object to damaging evidence because I don't want to call attention to it or exaggerate its importance. Juries tend to forget some of the testimony they hear, but not if the defense counsel makes an issue of it."

"I don't understand why you haven't interviewed the three of us. Isn't our testimony important?" Bishop Barieno asked. "I'm beginning to question your handling of our case."

"Gentlemen, as I told you before. You can fire me at any time. To answer your specific question, I have found no reason to interview you. To do so carries its own risks. If I need specific information that only you can give, I will ask. In the meantime it is in our mutual interest for me to concentrate on the prosecution's case and determine how I can best serve you."

"Well, I have to tell you," Bishop Courteer broke in, his pallor grayer than usual, "none of us is very comfortable with the way things are going."

"I'm sure it's not a pleasant experience," Kobs replied. "Have you heard anything in the testimony so far that is not true to the facts? Have you heard any witness testify to something that is refutable?"

Sandes avoided a direct response. "They make it sound as if we could have done things differently."

"You mean it wasn't possible for you to 'do things differently'?" Kobs asked.

"You wouldn't understand," Sandes said. "You've never walked in a bishop's shoes. Sometimes we are called to obey higher laws."

"Now that interests me," Kobs replied. "Just how would you explain that to a jury?"

"That's your job."

Kobs studied the man thoughtfully. "Yes it is," he said at last. "Do you gentlemen have any other concerns?"

The bishops were mute.

"In that case, Marcie and David will pick the three of you up at your hotel at eight tomorrow morning. We want you to understand the entire legal system. They will give you something of an instructional tour. Please be prompt. Court reconvenes at one p.m."

"What sort of instructional tour?" Barieno asked.

"Let it be a surprise," Kobs replied.

Goulding stood, half-facing the witness and half toward the jury. The witness, an attractive young assistant district attorney, responded to questions about her qualifications before Goulding asked, "Were you the prosecutor at the trial of the Reverend Roscoe Dempsey?"

"I was."

"Was Dempsey a priest of the diocese of Colchester?"

"Technically, no. He was a priest of the Palm Sands, Florida diocese. Bishop Barieno transferred him on loan to the Colchester diocese."

"Did the jury convict Dempsey on charges of sexual abuse of minors?"

"No, the trial never got that far. Dempsey confessed when confronted with the boys' testimony."

"Describe for the jury the nature of the sexual abuse to which he confessed."

The murmuring courtroom hushed.

"Dempsey used the confessional to identify boys who were experimenting with their sexuality by masturbating. He would call them to the rectory at some later time, slap them about as a kind of penance for their sins of masturbation, and then 'teach them' — his words — about sex.

He would fellate or masturbate them by hand and have them do the same to him. On some instances he would violently sodomize them. He would berate them for leading a priest of God into sin, and then give them absolution."

"Dempsey is now in prison."

"Yes. The judge sentenced him to twenty years."

"Was Dempsey ever accused of sexual abuse in his home diocese?"

"Yes, in the sense that complaints were made to Bishop Barieno."

"Was he prosecuted there?"

"No, he was not."

"Did Bishop Barieno know that Dempsey was a pedophile before transferring him to Sandes?"

"Yes."

"How do you know this?"

"In his confession at the trial, Dempsey said that early in his history of abuse he had told Barieno of his problem and had asked for help."

"Did that request occur in the context of a sacramental confession?"

"No, it occurred in the priest's rectory on the occasion of a visit by Barieno."

"What was Barieno's response to Dempsey's request?"

"He sympathized with Dempsey, but told him the only help he needed was to pray more and avoid the occasions of sin."

"Did Bishop Barieno ever notify the authorities?"

"No."

"Did Bishop Sandes know at the time of the transfer that Dempsey was a pedophile?"

"Yes."

"How do you know that?"

"Barieno had e-mailed the man's entire history. Investigators found the message on both Barieno's and Sandes's personal computers."

"Were credible allegations of sexual abuse made against Dempsey in Sandes's diocese?"

"Yes, but at first only to the bishop."

"Did Bishop Sandes notify the police?"

"Never."

"Thank you. No further questions." Goulding submitted as exhibits the record of the partial trial, the confession of Reverend Dempsey, and a copy of the e-mail from Bishop Barieno to Bishop Sandes. To Kobs: "Your witness."

Kobs reached out for his copies of the exhibits. "No questions."

DEENAH

Come on, Deenah. Deal with the facts. I remember the day I heard that Father Bruce was no longer at the parish. He simply disappeared. It was because of health problems the neighbors said. I breathed again, but the memories keep coming back. Why can't I just forget it?

Then mama decided that what I needed was to see a really *holy* priest. I didn't want to, but mama thought a new assistant at the parish was really something. He made everyone laugh during his sermons. He was charismatic, she told me. I took that to mean handsome.

By then I was fourteen and a freshman in the public high school. I was anxious all the time and afraid to make friends among my classmates. I was afraid to even talk with them. I would go to school in the morning and come home right after my last class. And at home I stayed in my room. I wouldn't have gone to school, but my parents made me. I still skipped church on Sunday. I'd tell my parents that I had to go to a different Mass.

I remember how my body was changing then. My breasts were larger than my classmates were. I felt ugly, and kept wanting to die. I'd imagine myself dying from an incurable disease and that my parents would be sorry.

Mama finally talked me into seeing this new priest, Father Dan. I was turning fifteen then. He had a nice apartment in the rectory with a kind of office-living room combination. Up close he looked really young. He had curly black hair and a nice smile. At first we just talked about little things. He'd make me laugh. I got to like him.

Mama had told him about Father Bruce and one day he talked about what that priest had done to me. "What he did was very wrong," he said. "What you did to him should not worry you anymore. It's over. You were just a child then. We'll work together to make you feel good about yourself again. Would you like to do that?"

For months I met with him every week for an hour or so. We didn't talk about Father Bruce unless I brought it up. Father Dan made me laugh and feel special. I can remember his exact words.

"You are special, Deenah. You are very special to me. I know that God has sent you to me as a very special gift."

By then I had such a crush on him. I couldn't wait to see him each week. One day he did bring up Father Bruce again.

"Do you think the past is gone for you, Deenah?" he asked. "Are you still troubled by what Father Bruce did to you?"

I said I had almost forgotten Father Bruce.

"Good," he said, "because God wants me to teach you how to feel good about yourself. You don't need to dwell on ugly things. You are beautiful, and you are special, and God wants me to teach you just how beautiful and special you are."

Something in the back of my head didn't seem right, but I was thrilled that he thought I was beautiful. No one had ever told me that, not even Mama. My feelings of being ugly began to go away. His smile was so gentle, his eyes so caring.

"Are you ready to begin?" he asked.

I nodded, yes.

The first lessons were all about relaxing. He had me sit in a big leather recliner with my feet up and my eyes closed.

"Breathe deep regular breaths," he said. "Feel your body getting heavier and heavier with each breath. Signal me with a twitch of your right index finger when you feel the weight of your body against the chair and a real heaviness."

It took me a while at first, but after a time I twitched my finger.

"Now I want you to imagine yourself on an elevator that will take you deeper and deeper to a special place. When it stops you will see a door. Go through the door. You will find yourself on a beautiful beach. When you get there twitch your finger."

It didn't take me too long.

"You are alone and you are naked. Feel the warm sun and a warm, soothing wind on your body. It feels good to be naked. You feel good. You feel good about being Deenah. You feel good about being naked Deenah. You feel beautiful. You are alone with nature. Isn't it beautiful?"

I twitched my finger.

He went through the same lesson every meeting for weeks, finally telling me to imagine any scene I wanted where I felt comfortable being naked. I just loved those lessons.

One day he said, "I want you to imagine yourself on your private beach again. But this time you have invited someone to be with you. You picture yourself with him. You are both naked. You swim, and toss a beach ball, and run on the sand. Tell me when you have that scene in your imagination and are comfortable with yourself."

It didn't take me long to twitch my finger. I was getting good at relaxation. When he finally had me open my eyes, he asked me to tell him who I imagined my companion to be. "You," I answered.

"You are so sweet and special," he told me, and he gave me a hug.

He smelled so good, a spicy smell. Later I kept reliving that hug. The next week he seemed really glad to see me.

"Here, Deenah, this week we're going to celebrate." He handed me a glass. "It's wine," he said.

It made me feel warm all over. I drank it very slowly.

"Were you able to image what I looked like naked?" he asked.

"Maybe a little."

"I think you trust me, don't you, Deenah?"

"Oh, yes."

"Then I must trust you. If we're going to be equal friends I have to trust you as much as you trust me. Come with me."

He led me to his bedroom.

"We'll get naked together," he said. "You take off a piece of my clothing, and then I'll take off one of yours. We'll go until we're both naked."

He had me caress his naked body, and he caressed mine. He smelled so good.

"Lie beside me," he said.

He began to kiss and caress my face and then my breasts.

"Kiss me back."

I did. I kissed him hard.

And then he came on top of me. He guided my knees up around him, and came inside.

"Is it okay to do this?" I asked.

"This will help you heal."

ROELLY

Paul Roelly, dressed for school, enters the kitchen and finds his mother at the table. His dog, Schotzy, rises slowly from the floor, comes and rubs his body against his leg.

"I thought you guys were leaving early for the trial," he says.

"We're running a little late," she replies, giving him a wide smile. "Your dad had to run to the office for a few minutes. I expect him any minute. Toast and eggs? There's donuts on top of the fridge."

"I'll eat a donut as I walk," he answers. "You guys have a good day."

"You too, hon." she replies. Her brow furrows as she looks into his spiritless eyes. "By the way, Dad and I are waiting for you to decide what you want for your birthday. It's less than a week away, and we want to make your eighteenth special."

"I'm working on it, Mom."

School is a mile straight down Division Street. He walks the street slowly for about a third of a mile, then turns. A few blocks bring him to the park where he sits on a bench, munches absently on the donut, and remembers the fun of Little League. He recalls his first home run, but the feeling of excitement doesn't come with the memory. *What did fun feel like?* he asks himself.

Fifteen minutes later he walks the length of St. Sebastian's parish: playground, grade school, rectory, and church. The leering image of Father Vincent Barieno returns, as does the memory of the first rape. It became a pattern. Barieno would call his teacher, and the nun would send the boy to the rectory. She didn't know she was sending him to be sodomized.

He couldn't tell anyone then. The priest ordered him to be silent. Besides that, his parents idolized Barieno. He thought they would believe the priest before him. When he could take it no longer, he just started skipping school. Even though they punished him, he still refused to go, either to school or to church. Eventually they transferred him to the public school. By then he had lost a year. His grades kept slipping. A counselor finally got the story out of him and together they told his parents.

Paul checks his watch. His parents would be gone by now so he retraces his steps and enters their home. Schotzy sidles up to him, tail wagging. Paul drops a note onto the table.

Dear Mom and Dad,

Don't worry about me. I'm not worth it.

Love, Paul

"I've got stuff to do, Schotzy," he says, bending and rubbing behind the dog's ears. He goes through the kitchen and into the attached garage. There he takes a length of flexible tubing kept for emergency sump pump needs and pushes one end onto the tail pipe of his mom's fourteen-year-old car, the other end through a side window which he rolls tight against the tube to secure it.

Schotzy begins to bark. Paul waits for a minute but the barking continues. Heaving a deep sigh, the boy opens the door. "Okay, Schotzy, come." He enters the driver's side of the car, helps the dog into the car and holds him in his lap. "Maybe you'll be running like you used to, Schotzy, when we get to where we're going. And maybe I'll be happy again."

Paul turns the key and buries his face in Schotzy's fur.

Chapter Seven

BISHOP BARIENO

That Barieno was unable to keep his mind on the trial was especially true when the evidence mounted against his own behavior. The spin given the evidence by the prosecutor proved too uncomfortable. Unable to tolerate discomfort, Barieno was nonetheless habitually irritated. It was enjoyment to him, but only when he directed it outward. Incoming irritation was another matter.

His eyes wandered and he passed judgment on all the people who fell within the scope of his vision. No one graded high, particularly Judge Monroe. Women didn't belong in positions where judgment was required, certainly not where judgment was passed on men.

The entire scene was just too tedious. Tedium! Tedium! Tedium! Tedium! he thought. He let his imagination transport pleasant memories and images to block out the moment's reality. Ipanema images took center stage: The two men filled comfortable lounge chairs on a fifth floor balcony of the Savoy. They sipped margaritas as they looked out over the expanse of Ipanema beach and the cobalt hues of the Atlantic. Paddy looked his sixty years. The generation-younger Barieno was a much less portly man than the one now reminiscing.

"Vinny, if your skin gets any redder, you won't need red apparel," Paddy commented.

"I'll be okay. I'm done sunbathing for this trip. Speaking of red,

I see that the Palm Sands diocese is still open," Barieno said, as he refilled their glasses.

"Enough for me," Paddy replied as the refill reached the half-glass mark. "I'm working on Palm Sands. You can never quite trust these Romans, but the nuncio assures me that you're in, that it's in the pipeline."

"Thanks for that. I love this kind of climate, and Palm Sands has it."

"You're welcome. You've been a loyal associate."

"I've been meaning to ask. I hope you plan to invite Bob, Wilbur, and me to Rome next month when they make you a cardinal."

"You three will be first on the list," Paddy said. "Now, I think I'll have one more swallow and then take a nap. Tonio will be here at nine this evening with our delectables."

"I don't understand Bob and Wilbur. They don't partake."

"I'm not sure about Bob. He might be finding it in the gay bars," Paddy said. "As for Wilbur, he says it's just not his thing. I told him that's fine as long as he doesn't blackmail the rest of us." He laughed. "I'm not worried. I've got both Bob's and Wilbur's names in the hopper."

"I'll get out of here," Barieno said. "You get your rest. You don't want to disappoint a girl from Ipanema." He left the balcony singing: "a girl for you and a boy for me. Dah, dah, dum, how happy we will be."

DONALD ABRUZZI

This old building doesn't have all the comforts of the main prison, but at least the cell is large enough and there's a place to store these toilet items. The warden said this place will be safe for me, even if it is a part of the old prison. He said that only inmates threatened by other inmates are housed here.

God, I was scared. I can still smell that huge guy sticking his grizzled face inches from mine. And all those other inmates caging me in so there was no place to run. What did he say? Oh, yeah.

"You're dead meat, priest. We don't let kid fuckers live with us. We've got some pride."

Just about wet my pants. The guards stopped it. I appealed to them and they investigated. Thank God for that. They took it to the warden. He said I'd be safe here. I wish I felt safe.

How could I have been so stupid? So many young girls before. I just lost control, no condom, taking that little redhead in the sanctuary. Stupid! Stupid! Stupid! Even more stupid was letting the kid escape before I could guarantee her silence. It would have been so simple to use those tested threats to shut her up. I bet I looked silly trying to catch her, stumbling on the altar steps, my pants still halfway down.

The little wretch. What was her name? Running home and squealing to her parents. Damn parents. Took the kid to the hospital and met the police there. The whole damn process went fast. They took a DNA sample from me and it matched the semen found in the girl. Damn, damn, damn. A life sentence.

I didn't go down without a fight though. I know something about the art of intimidation. I scared the hell out of Barieno. "Get me top-notch lawyers, by God, or I'll put our whole group out to the public."

In court, my lawyers portrayed the parents of the girl as contemptible, sophisticated pimps, and the little eight-year-old as a precocious, seductive whore. It didn't work. It wasn't enough to counter the DNA evidence and sway the jury. Damn! At least Barieno is intimidated enough to pay for an appeal. Maybe they can still find a way to get me out of here.

That little redhead was something else. Just picturing her gets me aroused. Sit on the bunk. Get the zipper down. Ah. Ah.

What's that noise? Zip up. Somebody's coming out of the shower room over there. What's he got in his hand? Looks like a piece of pipe. He's coming toward my cell. Thank God for the bars. Oh my God. He pushed the door open. It wasn't locked. What's he doing? Looks like he took a piece of tape from the lock. What? He's eating the tape. That horrible grin! Hard to breathe. "Stay back! Guards! Guards!" I can't yell any louder. "No, don't. I'll pay you. Anything. No. Please don't. Ugh!"

Kobs faced David and Marcie in the hallway outside the federal courtroom. "We didn't have time to talk about this before the trial re-opened this morning. Did our esteemed clients enjoy their instructional tour?"

"I don't think so," David replied, his brown eyes twinkling.

"Good old understated David," Marcie said. "They hated it. I think they came away unnerved. They don't show it, but I know it."

"Tell me about it," Kobs said.

"Mr. Harding, the warden, met us at the gate and conducted the tour himself. How did you ever work that?" Marcie asked.

"We were classmates," Kobs said, "and I've done a few favors for him."

"You describe it, David."

"Okay, Marcie. To begin the tour, Mr. Harding gave us a quick introduction to how convicts are admitted to the prison. Then he took us into the locked areas."

"Bang! The metal door clanged shut. I was watching the bishops," Marcie interjected. "It really startled them. Oh," she looked at David, "sorry David. You tell it."

"We started walking through the cell tiers," David said. "Some of the inmates recognized the bishops, evidently from either TV or newspaper coverage of the trial. Barieno went over to one cell and tried to engage the convict in friendly conversation. The guy spit in his face. Then we started to hear catcalls and whistles."

Marcie broke in. "One guy shouted out, 'Checking it out, bishops? Will it be comfy enough for you?'"

"I remember some of what they yelled," David said. 'We don't want you here. You belong in Andersonville. You belong in the gas chamber. You belong in hell. Come to this prison and we'll see that you get there.'"

"How did the bishops respond?" Kobs asked.

"It's hard to tell," David replied. "Their faces always look frozen. I really can't be sure what they were feeling."

"It's like they'd had Botox injections all over their face," Marcie said.

"The convicts frightened me," David said.

"Wimp," Marcie teased.

"How do you know about Botox?" David teased back.

"Go on," Kobs said.

David continued. "Toward the end of the tour, the warden stopped by an open and empty cell, about the only empty one we saw there. He invited the bishops to step inside. They went in first. I stepped back to let Marcie go in before me, and she slammed the door on them. The warden left to get someone to reopen the cell. The bishops just stared out at us. Like before, they showed no facial change, but I think I saw fear in their eyes."

"Me too," Marcie said.

"They may not show it, but one thing bishops are able to feel is fear," Kobs said. He shoved a newspaper across the table and pointed to a minor headline. "Do you recognize that name?"

"Abruzzi! Why he's one of the seven pedophiles the prosecution's case is built on. One of the points of conspiracy," David said.

"He's one of the three from Barieno's diocese," Marcie said.

"Murdered! How's that for coincidence? It says here that another inmate got him with a piece of pipe in his own cell. The cell was locked when the guards got there. They can't figure out how the killer got in. When they arrived he was sitting on the bunk and the corpse was on the floor. The guy was grinning at the guards. He figured his stock would go up with the other inmates. Guards say it will."

"The time has come to hit our clients with reality," Kobs said. "We'll meet at the office after court adjourns this afternoon."

In his precise and deliberate manner Goulding led the witness, an assistant district attorney from Palm Sands, through certain details of Donald Abruzzi's trial. "You said Abruzzi was convicted of raping a young girl?"

"Correct."

"Is this Donald Abruzzi the same man who was murdered in prison just the other day?"

"Yes, he is."

"Where did the rape occur?"

"In the sanctuary of the church where he served as pastor."

"How old was the little girl?"

"She was eight years old."

Goulding waited for the gasps and other sounds of shock in the audience begin to abate. "Did Bishop Barieno know prior to that rape that Abruzzi was a pedophile?"

"Yes, he did."

"How do you know that?"

"There are several proofs. For one, Abruzzi had a prior conviction for child molestation. At that trial he was permitted to confess to a lesser charge and was sentenced to a probation period of several years."

"Did he serve that probationary time in a parish?"

"Yes."

"Was he sent there by Barieno?"

"Yes."

"You mentioned more than one proof."

"A priest of the Palm Sands chancery office testified that Bishop Barieno had openly discussed Abruzzi's pedophilic activity several years before the rape at a meeting of upper-tier chancery staff. That testimony was confirmed under oath by other attendees of the meeting."

"Are there any other indications that Bishop Barieno knew Donald Abruzzi to be a pedophile, yet continued to harbor him?"

"Yes. Before the police arrested Abruzzi, Barieno transferred him to Bishop Sandes's diocese, Colchester. When the police came there looking, Sandes sent him to Courteer's diocese, San Miguel. The police finally caught up with Abruzzi on a ship about to sail to Africa. Bishop Barieno's signature was on the check that purchased Abruzzi's passage to Africa."

"Thank you. No further questions." To Kobs: "your witness."

Kobs, studying the jury, gave a casual shrug of his shoulders. "No questions."

With Marcie and David at his side, Kobs sat across from the three bishops at a circular table in one of the smaller conference rooms at the law firm. Kobs opened the meeting with the ingenuous question: "How do you gentlemen feel about the progress of the trial?"

"You tell us," Sandes responded. "I think we're getting creamed."

"How about you two?" Kobs asked calmly, nodding at Courteer and Barieno.

"I'd agree with Bishop Sandes," Courteer said. "Even though the prosecution hasn't started on me as yet."

"And you?" Kobs asked Barieno.

"Before we get to that," Barieno answered testily, "I want to tell you I did not appreciate that prison tour one bit. What was that supposed to prove?"

"It proves nothing at all," Kobs said. "I felt it important to have you gentlemen experience the complete legal system. Don't tell me that you didn't get the real feel of prison life."

"I don't need to feel what it's like," Barieno said angrily. "And I don't need you to give me lessons in anything."

"Nor I," Sandes said, clearly agitated.

Kobs looked each of them in the eyes, moving from one to another. "Yes, you do," he said. "That's where you're going to spend twenty years or more of your lives. Either there or at another federal prison."

"Are you saying that you are unable to defend us?" Sandes snapped.

"No, I didn't say that."

"What exactly do you mean?" Barieno asked, his eyes wide.

"I mean I can't refute the prosecution's evidence. Goulding is proving beyond any possibility of refutation that you are guilty of the charges against you."

"I knew we should have fired you after hearing that first witness. Now that they've got a noose around our necks, you're copping out." Sandes turned to Barieno. "It looks like we got suckered into hiring the B team."

Kobs let the insult pass. "I'm not copping out, as you put it. I'm simply telling you the truth. That's part of my job. I cannot, nor could any defense attorney I know, defend you on your not guilty pleas when the evidence against you is so overwhelming."

"Are you now suggesting that we plead guilty? Throw ourselves on the mercy of the court?" Courteer asked.

"No, not at all. I don't think you'd find any mercy from Judge

Monroe on a guilty plea. She has a contrary reputation, one that hands down heavy sentences. I should add that the prosecution is not amenable to having you plead to a lesser charge. Goulding believes he has you tied up in damning evidence."

"I'm getting lost here," Sandes growled. "What exactly are you getting at?"

"I do suggest that you change your plea," Kobs replied. "Not to a guilty plea, but to not guilty by reason of mental defect." He settled back in his chair and waited for his words to take effect.

"You're asking us to plead insanity?" Sandes blustered, standing up and leaning across the table. "The only thing insane here is that idea."

"Besides, that would be a lie." Courteer added.

"No one would believe it!" Barieno said.

"I believe it," Kobs replied.

"Why didn't you tell us all this at the beginning?" Sandes demanded, still on his feet.

"For two reasons. One, at that time I didn't have this argument in order. And two, you would not have agreed. You needed to hear the evidence and you needed the truth. I wasn't ready, and neither were you."

"I find the whole idea repellent," Sandes said. He sat down.

Kobs looked at them one by one, waiting to meet their eyes.

After a considerable spell of silence, Sandes asked, "How do you see our chances if we change our plea?"

"Reasonably good," Kobs said. "There are never guarantees before a jury with so much evidence before them, but I believe I can argue forcefully that your new plea is the most reasonable conclusion for them to make."

"Can you tell us how you will argue it?" Courteer asked.

"Yes. How will you prove we're *insane*?" Barieno grumbled.

"I wouldn't use the word insane with you gentlemen. I may with the jury, but not with you. Have you ever heard the legal term mens rea?"

"My Latin isn't that good any more," Sandes said.

"It literally means guilty mind," Kobs said. "Generally, in law, a person who does not perceive that a criminal act is morally wrong will not be charged or convicted of the crime. You have been charged under the prosecution's perception that you did have a mens rea. Let me ask you this. Did you feel guilty of a criminal action when you did what you did?"

"Of course not" Sandes replied.

"That's what you had in mind when you told me I'd never walked in a bishop's shoes, isn't it?" Kobs asked.

"Yes, something like that."

"There you are then! That gives you some idea of how I intend to proceed. Of course there will be more to the argument than that. We will need to show that your lack of mens rea doesn't flow from either ignorance or from evil, and that it stems from a mental defect. There will be objections from the prosecution. I will have to overcome them."

"What's the next step here?" Sandes asked.

"That will be for you to change your plea. When we enter that plea, Judge Monroe will probably call me on the carpet. I'll take that hit. The prosecution will throw a fit, claiming that I am only trying to delay the trial."

"Is delay good?"

"Normally, yes. In our case, I don't think so." Kobs stood. "Let's stop here for a coffee break. David? Marcie?"

The room was quiet as David refilled coffee cups and Marcie offered cream, sugar, and scones. Eyes turned to Courteer as he made an elaborate ritual of sugar first, cream last.

Kobs resumed the conversation. "Goulding will ask for time to have you each checked out by the prosecution's psychiatrists."

"I suppose you will want us to go into those psychiatric sessions and cackle and babble like idiots?" Barieno asked.

"No. I expect that you will do the opposite, that you will not lie, and that you will act normally. They will in turn testify in court that you are perfectly sane."

"Then, I assume you will have psychiatrists who will argue that we are nuts," Barieno grumbled.

"We will have an array of experts, yes," Kobs replied.

"So it boils down to a battle between experts," Sandes said.

"Not exactly. It boils down to a battle between Goulding and myself for the minds of the jury. Ultimately it will be for the jury, not the experts, to decide if you suffer from a mental defect."

"What happens to us if you convince the jury?" Courteer asked, sipping coffee, pinky extended.

"First, you *don't* go to prison. Next, Judge Monroe will have to determine how best to deal with your mental defect so as to insure that you have been cured. The usual way would be to send you to a hospital that specializes in mental disorders until you are declared free of your malady."

"But the prosecution's psychiatrists will already have declared that we are sane. You said so yourself."

"There you are then. The prosecution's own expert witnesses will judge you to be sane. Only a jury with no special expertise in the psychological sciences will decide otherwise. You tell me, gentlemen, how long it would take men of your abilities to convince the experts in that facility to agree with their professional peers and disagree with the jury?" Kobs's white-toothed smile beamed from its red stubble frame.

"How will you argue this mens rea and other stuff?" Courteer asked.

"I'm working on that. But, trust me, you won't like it."

"I have to think about this," Sandes said. "When do you need our answer?"

"The sooner the better. Goulding might rest the prosecution any day."

"What if we don't agree?" Barieno asked.

"Then I will tell the jury what nice fellows you are in twenty or more ways. The jury will still find you guilty as charged. When it comes time for your sentencing, I'll repeat all those nice things, bring in an assortment of your friends to agree with me, and leave you in the hands of Judge Monroe. I expect she'll sentence you to a minimum of twenty years, one year for each of those nice things I said about you."

After the bishops left, Marcie looked at Kobs. "Aren't we dealing with strict liability laws in this case? Aren't these guys guilty of conspiracy in child rape and sodomy? I thought mens rea didn't apply."

"It doesn't, Marcie. That's only the first step on the way. But it's one the bishops could understand. It sets the direction. After that we will be walking into uncharted territory. Here's my thinking. I want your reaction, yours too, David. We need to get our experts lined up and subpoenas out —"

Chapter Eight

Bill Goulding looked across his desk into the bland face of FBI Agent Kurt Miller.

"Don't tell me you've come up with something."

"Something!" Miller smiled.

"It may be too late," Goulding said. "If things go as planned I will rest the prosecution in a week or less. But, let's have it."

"What we've found ties in with what I've already given you. These three bishops were classmates in the seminary, Roman trained, and high on the list of Cardinal Brendan O'Connell's favorites. He made them all bishops. What's new is that the four of them often vacationed together."

"By four, you mean Barieno, Courteer, Sandes, *and* O'Connell?"

"Right. *And* O'Connell."

"Okay. So?"

"So, they vacationed together at least annually. They always flew to Rio de Janeiro. They stayed in a luxurious hotel off the beach at Ipanema. Their rooms looked down on the beach and the Atlantic. Very pricey digs."

"So?"

"They shed their uniforms before they got there, and registered at the hotel using only their names, not their titles."

"Go on."

"They always vacationed there during *Carnaval.*"

"What's that?"

"It precedes Lent, much like our Mardi Gras here in the U.S., only it lasts longer and far exceeds Mardi Gras in extravagance. It's a riotous, fun-loving time of unrestrained frolicking: dancing in the streets, spectacular parades like that of the samba schools, and the drag queen parade."

"Were these four involved in unrestrained frolicking?"

"It appears that way. My contacts in Rio followed a trail that led to a man named Tonio. Tonio was a significant contact for the four. At that time O'Connell was an archbishop and the other three were monsignors. Tonio is a pimp. As it turned out, his code of silence was easily breached. Per Tonio, he provided sexual partners for these men."

"All of them?"

"We are only sure about O'Connell and Barieno."

"What kind of sexual partners?"

"Young boys for Barieno. For O'Connell, the partners took the form of well-proportioned and pretty young adult girls. He referred to each as his 'girl from Ipanema.' You probably remember the song."

"What about Sandes and Courteer?"

"My contact found nothing. Tonio never supplied them. Nor could the contact find any indication that they took to sexual escapades. By the way, Tonio would be only too willing to testify. I'm told a free trip to the U.S. would be sufficient enticement for him to do so."

Goulding was silent for a time, running the information through the design of his prosecution strategy. "It all speaks to motive," he said at last. "If these guys find every kind of sex acceptable for themselves, it implies they can find pedophilic sex acceptable in their subordinates."

Goulding stood and paced back and forth behind his desk. "But! A major but! For it to be of value, we would have to show that Sandes and Courteer at least knew of the sexual activity of the others and found it acceptable. A motive for some, but not for all doesn't help us. If they didn't know about it, the motive doesn't apply to them. The whole thing becomes relevant to the trial only if we are forced into producing a reasonable motive. Right now, the facts themselves are doubly damning and should convict on their own merit."

He was silent again. "Also," he said, "Jim Kobs would trample that pimp Tonio into the dust under cross-examination. If I know Kobs, he is in a diligent search for an opening that lets him obfuscate the evidence and bury it under a cloud of imaginative alternatives. No. I appreciate the information, Kurt, but I won't use it except as a last resort."

"Do you want me to keep going on Sandes and Courteer?" Kurt asked.

"Sure, if you can afford the time. If you get something that proves they all found any kind of sex acceptable we would have a reasonable explanation of how they could tolerate that kind of activity among their priests."

"Okay. What about O'Connell?"

"I think I just may depose O'Connell."

DEENAH

If I'm honest with myself, I loved being his lover. I felt so grown up. I was sure he loved me, and I'd spend hours daydreaming about our being together sometime. Even if he was a priest, he'd work it out. He even said so. "I'll always love you, Deenah."

We met for over three years, usually every Wednesday evening. And we'd make love whenever it wasn't my time. We even had special signals for special times. If he gave me a left-handed wave after Mass on Sunday, it meant we'd meet that afternoon.

We never went anywhere together, though. He said it was too dangerous.

"It would be obvious to anyone that we're in love," he said.

"People would see it."

I'll never forget it. We were having a special Sunday afternoon together. I went from full to empty in an instant.

"We have to talk," he said after we had made love. We were sitting in the recliners in his office. He had served us mixed nuts and wine.

"I love to hear you talk," I said.

"This is serious talk, Deenah. I have a confession to make. I've been selfish. I've wanted you all to myself, and only thought about me. But it's my job to think about you. I can't be selfish any longer. You need someone wiser than me to take you to the next level. You can go further, and it will take a more experienced teacher."

"I don't understand," I stammered.

"Trust me."

"I thought we loved each other."

"Sometimes love asks hard things from us. I want you to see Father Campbell. I'll set it up for you."

"I won't!"

"You'll do as I say!"

I ran out, sobbing. I've never hurt like that. I think I cried for days. When it came time for our next regular meeting, I walked to the rectory, hoping he'd talk to me, hoping he hadn't meant it. I was half a block away when I saw her walk up to the rectory door. I knew her. She was a freshman at the high school. I was a senior then, but I knew her. We had talked. She was beautiful. When she rang the bell, I saw Father Dan at the door, smiling and drawing her in. I knew then, it was over. I was being replaced. A few years from then she'd be standing where I was.

I'm still empty. And I can't stop these tears. I could never talk to anyone about it, certainly not to my parents. I was confused and ashamed. I didn't go to college, and I've had a number of jobs. I did finally go to a therapist, and she is helping me. I'll see her again after the trial. I just feel like dumb Deenah.

JACOB

That nice couple who sat to my right have not been here for several days. Roelly, they said their name was. They had to spell it for me. I hope they're okay. They told me they had a young son who was abused. I wonder how young he was.

I was only seven years old when Father Al brought Buddy, Gus, and me here to the city to see the Cubs play a doubleheader. At the game he treated us to Coke and hot dogs. Afterward he took us all to a motel for the night.

I could never recall what time of night he woke me up. After fondling my genitals he sodomized me. I didn't even know that word then. I had already made my First Confession and First Communion so I knew what he meant when he said I couldn't tell anybody because of the seal of confession. If I ever told anyone, he said, I would go to hell and so would Buddy and Gus. He was teaching me about sex, he said, about the way grown-ups act.

When we got home the next day, Buddy asked me if Father Al had "done it" to me. I knew what he meant. I was hesitant, but I nodded yes. Buddy said he'd done it to him and also to Gus. Buddy was eleven then. He said he didn't care if he would go to hell. He was going to tell Mom and Dad. And he did. Then so did Gus, who was nine. When Mom and Dad asked me, I was afraid, but I told them the truth. I've never told anyone since. I didn't want ever again to see the hurt I saw in Mom's eyes, or the steely fire in Dad's.

They never told us boys what they did about it. Father Al left our parish soon after that. They called it a routine transfer. I learned later that he was transferred to another parish at the other end of the diocese. Dad was subpoenaed by the attorneys for the diocese. As a young adult, I learned that Dad was deposed and that depositions are public documents. I got a copy of the deposition. Those attorneys crucified Dad. They questioned Dad and Mom's ability to be good parents. As if they were the ones at fault. They insinuated that we boys were the instigators.

Dad left the church and took us all with him. We boys were taken out of Catholic school and put in the public school. For a long time we didn't attend any church, but later we joined the Lutheran church. Mom sank into a deep depression. As long as I live, I will never forget her gradual descent into that emotional hell. I can see her now, sitting at Sunday services in the Lutheran church, rosary in hand, and staring blank-eyed into space. In the end, it killed her. She was forty-one and institutionalized when she died. I was only twelve.

We boys survived, all with the help of Dad and a therapist. Buddy finally won a battle with the bottle. Gus went through several marriages before he settled down. I was probably too young to take in the full horror of what was done to me, but not so young that it hasn't been with me every day since it happened. Forgiveness is a goal we are all called to achieve. And I think I can forgive what that man did to me. But, how do you forgive the trail of wounds that festered year after year in every member of my family?

Oh my, that pretty girl next to me has tears flowing and she's trying to wipe them away with the tips of her fingers. "Would you like to have these tissues?"

"Oh, yes. Thank you."

She has pretty eyes. They met mine in a kind of friendly connection. This trial gets boring after a while. Piece by piece, I can see the prosecutor build his case. But I can't stay with it. Goulding is holding up a graph. It's the same size as that sign at the hotel that announced a retirement party for Father Al.

Inez and I were staying at that same hotel here in the city. We had taken a three-day weekend to celebrate our third anniversary.

My engineering work was gathering speed about then. I remember waiting for Inez by the stairs in the lobby when Father Al walked by. He stopped and looked at me.

"You're Jacob. I heard your mother died a few years back."

"Yes, she did. Thirteen years ago." I tried to keep emotion from my voice.

"In a mental institution, I heard."

I nodded.

"That's God's punishment on you boys for squealing."

I could have killed him there, but grabbed a railing to keep myself steady. "You cold, murdering son of a bitch," I roared as he walked on.

I started to cry then, thinking of the good, loving woman my mother had been. And how she was destroyed by this man's breach of trust. He won't hold a candle to Mom at judgment time.

"Are you all right?" Inez stood on the steps looking at me.

"I'm fine. Just got something in my eye," I'd said. "Let's go celebrate."

Calm down now, Jacob. Remember your heart.

The testimony was crisp and to the point. Hans Flascher was a priest of Barieno's diocese whom Barieno had transferred to Courteer's jurisdiction after a flurry of sexual-abuse allegations were made to the bishop. Assigned to a parish by Courteer, Flascher soon ingratiated himself into the company of young parents. He grew particularly close to the parents of a young boy and girl.

Finding it difficult to locate a babysitter on an occasion when they had tickets to a traveling Broadway production, the parents mentioned the fact in casual conversation while entertaining the priest at dinner one evening. He volunteered at once.

Flascher arrived on time and was briefed on the location of necessities. Dinner was ready in the oven. All he need do was serve it to himself and the children. He should leave the dishes unwashed. The parents had already bathed the children. Customary bedtime for the girl, the younger of the two children, was eight o'clock, for the boy eight thirty. The parents left, the wife giving Flascher a grateful peck on the cheek.

On arrival at the theater they were informed of a brief delay in the performance. After taking their seats the announcement was made that the musical was cancelled. The performers' flight had at first been delayed, then cancelled because of weather. They returned home, arriving shortly after nine.

Not wanting to wake the children, they entered the home silently. Flascher was not in the living room. Hearing sounds in the boy's bedroom, they opened the door. Flascher was in the act of anal copulation with the eight-year-old boy. The mother carried the crying boy out of the room and called the police. The father thrashed the priest to near unconsciousness.

When knowledge of Flascher's pending trial became public, the notoriety unleashed a flood of allegations against the priest heretofore publicly unknown. In his own diocese, Barieno had won the silence of parents by saying that their allegation against Flascher was the only one ever made against him. They were welcome to take legal action, but should be aware that the diocese would use every means available to defend the priest. No parent took action. Two formerly unknown complainants came forward in Courteer's diocese. He had successfully used Barieno's ploy on them.

Goulding produced six witnesses who testified that the bishops had certain knowledge of the priest's sexual behavior, and had done nothing to prevent its continuance.

BISHOP BARIENO

Barieno, tired of testimony and bored by the proceedings, took a small Sony Walkman from his briefcase, placed the hearing piece in his right ear, adjusted the volume, and listened — to his own voice. His imagination took him back to the scene of a packed cathedral in Palm Sands. Silence filled the huge nave except for the rich baritone sounds emanating from his own throat. In the expectant eyes of the throng, he read their eagerness for each twist of his homily. At its conclusion they rose as one, their applause echoing throughout the four great sections of the building's cruciform interior. He relived the final procession to the apse and felt again his elation from the homage accorded him there as the faithful passed by, stopping to kiss his ring.

Next Pentecost, he thought, I will celebrate the liturgy in the city's stadium and fill it with fifty thousand of the faithful. My procession will move from one end to the other. A parade of my knights will proceed ahead of me. I will wear a new red chasuble and stole from Gammarelli's in Rome. And, abolished or not, I will wear my gold-buckled red slippers. I will be the chief actor in the great drama of the Mass. It will be magnificent, simply magnificent. I will preach a homily to end all homilies. I will captivate my audience. I can hear their applause. I can smell my triumph and picture mobs reverencing my ring. If this wretched trial continues long, I will write the homily here.

Placing the Walkman back into his briefcase, he noticed the coffee stain on the white shirtsleeve protruding from his suit jacket. His irritation was immediate as he recalled the spill made by his breakfast waitress. He had given the hapless girl a royal reaming, calling her a clumsy peasant, too incompetent even for a servant position. "Do you know who I am?" he demanded. In the end she was reduced to tears. His relentless attack was an embarrassment to his companions. Something he failed to notice.

Looking aside at Sandes and Courteer, his thoughts swerved their way. Wilbur spends too much time on his building projects, he mused. For his pastoral responsibilities he should be the one on display, not some pile of bricks and mortar. The same goes for that bookworm, Courteer. He should get out of his library and put himself in front of the people. *Ubi Episcopus, ibi Ecclesia*, I say. Where the bishop is, there is the Church. God doesn't make bishops to hide behind buildings or books. And that's what I suggested to the papal nuncio recently. He nodded in reply. Assent, I was sure. Bob and Wilbur have come as far as they will go. For myself, I have higher roles waiting. Chicago should have gone to me, not to that mediocre Thompson. Hopefully L.A. or Philadelphia will open up soon.

I don't understand how so many priests could ever leave the clerical life. They will never have the status or be given the esteem and recognition they would get in the priesthood. Nor will they get the same rewards. Every year since my ordination as bishop, I have received a new Cadillac from admiring members of the faithful. One even donated twenty thousand dollars to purchase the ruby for my pontifical ring.

In my diocese I am the law. I make executive decisions and pass judgment. That's the way it should be. Here I am surrounded by little people, people incapable of judgment, arrogant little people like that Goulding. He keeps talking about, and lamenting, the injustice done to *victims* of sexual abuse. Who really are the victims? The real victims in this kangaroo court are the priests and their bishops. Those children whose lost innocence he laments are not so innocent. They are the real seducers. Don't kid yourself. Those twelve- and fourteen-year-olds are capable of a seductiveness that puts whores and male prostitutes to shame. They can wiggle their little butts to entice as effectively as any exotic dancer. I've experienced it. Let's put the blame where it truly lies. They should be the ones on trial here.

✠

Chapter Nine

ROELLY

Mike Roelly sat alone in the front of the courtroom. His eyes were red and underscored with pouches from weeping and loss of sleep. Too exhausted from the funeral and from grief, Mary did not return with her husband to the trial.

Mike watched the backs of the three bishops as they sat impassively at the defense counsel table. Do you guys have any clue to the devastation you bring to families? Do you give a damn?

Anger began to kindle and flame in him. When Barieno turned his face to look at the next advancing witness, Mike looked into his remote and remorseless eyes. The bishop turned back, yawning. Suddenly, white hot with rage Mike snapped. He stood up.

"Barieno, you buggered my son," he shouted. "Now you've killed him. Pedophile! Murderer!"

"Bailiff!" Judge Monroe called. "Remove that gentleman. I want to see him in my chambers. Mr. Goulding and Mr. Kobs, I want you there as well. Ladies and gentlemen of the jury, please return to the jury room. I will see you there shortly. You are to disregard this man's outburst."

Mike was sobbing uncontrollably as the bailiff, joined now by another deputy, escorted him firmly to the judge's chamber.

"I move for a mistrial," Kobs said.

"I'll rule on that later, Mr. Kobs," the judge replied and rose from the bench.

"What's your name, sir?" she asked when she, Mike, and the two attorneys were seated at a table.

"Michael Roelly, Your Honor," he replied, wiping tears away.

"Mr. Roelly, do you have any idea how your outburst might compromise the fairness of this trial?"

"I suppose I should apologize, Your Honor," Mike responded, still crying, "but I buried my eighteen-year-old son a few days ago. He took his own life. He's been depressed since he was abused by Barieno."

"At this point, Mr. Roelly, that's your allegation. Can you understand that?"

Mike nodded.

"If you have information that's pertinent to this trial, that testimony can only be presented through the prosecution by Mr. Goulding." She turned to the prosecutor.

"I'll have one of my staff depose Mr. Roelly," Goulding said

"Mr. Kobs, I'll rule on your motion when court reconvenes, and after I've talked to the jury."

An hour later the judge ruled from the bench. "Your motion for mistrial is denied, Mr. Kobs," she said. "After talking with the jury, I am convinced they are capable of ignoring Mr. Roelly's uninvited comments and can judge this case on the merits of the prosecution's presentation and your defense. Let's proceed."

CARDINAL O'CONNELL

VIDEO OPERATOR: We are now recording and on the record. My name is Samuel Berg, a certified legal video recorder for Chicago Legal Video Reporters, Inc.

Today is June 18, 2005. The time is 9:37 a.m. This is a deposition of Cardinal Brendan O'Connell in matters under scrutiny by the U.S. Attorney's Office and is being held at the U.S. Federal Building in Chicago. The court reporter is Samantha Williams of Chicago Legal Video Reporters, Inc. At this time counsel will state their names and the court reporter will administer the oath.

MR. GOULDING: I am Assistant U.S. Attorney William Goulding and I represent the U.S. Attorney's office.

MR. PILASTER: I am Attorney Jonas C. Pilaster and I represent His Eminence, Cardinal O'Connell.

MR. KOBS: I am Attorney James G. Kobs of the law firm Kobs, Mayer, and Guggenbuhl. I am currently representing Bishops Vincent Barieno, Wilbur Sandes, and Robert Courteer in matters that may be related to the testimony given here today.

MR. GOULDING: The parties stipulate that all objections except objections as to form are reserved to such time as this deposition may be used at trial.

MR. PILASTER: I object to this entire deposition on first amendment grounds. Any inquiry into the internal workings of the Roman Catholic Church is contrary to that amendment.

MR. GOULDING: We don't agree that the first amendment applies. However, we will proceed with the understanding that an objection has been made on first amendment grounds.

MR. PILASTER: As long as that is clearly understood.

SUMMARY: Mr. Goulding began a series of questions to the eighty-year-old cardinal, and obtained information as to the cardinal's name, date and place of birth, residence, retired status, citizenship, education, degrees, ordination as a priest, ministerial assignments, ordina-

tion as a bishop, installation as archbishop of Chicago, and his retirement. Then —

Q. Your Eminence, do you know Vincent Barieno?"
A. Yes, I do know Bishop Barieno.

Q. Will you please give a brief history of your relationship with
Barieno?
A. I knew Vincent Barieno when he was a bright seminarian for
the archdiocese. I sent him to Rome for his theology studies. After his
ordination to the priesthood, I assigned him to parish duties, and
then to further studies in canon law in Rome. On his return, I assigned him to the chancery, where he worked first in the marriage tribunal and then as chief of the personnel department.

Q. What is a marriage tribunal?
A. It's analogous to a court of law. Decisions are made there on
questions of marriage validity.

Q. Did you make Barieno a bishop?
A. Only the pope can do that.

Q. Did you recommend him for that office?
A. I did.

SUMMARY: At this point Goulding went through the history of
O'Connell's relationship to Sandes and Courteer. The histories were
identical to that of Barieno with minor exceptions, one being that
Courteer was made a bishop not from a chancery position, but from
that of a seminary rector.

Q. Prior to your retirement, all three of these men were under
your authority. Is that accurate?
A. That is correct.

Q. Did you ever receive an allegation of sexual misconduct against any of them?

A. Never.

Q. Never?

A. None that I recall.

Q. Your Eminence, I'm going to show you this letter. It's a letter from Mr. and Mrs. Michael Roelly alleging that Bishop Barieno, then Father Barieno, had sexually abused their son. Do you recall seeing that letter?

A. I don't remember that.

Q. Read the letter please. Perhaps that will refresh your memory.

A. I have no recollection of ever seeing this letter.

Q. Did you read all of the mail addressed to you?

A. No. Much of it was sent according to subject matter to the person responsible.

Q. I'm now going to show you another letter. Is that your signature on the letter?

A. Yes, it is my signature.

Q. Read the letter please. Did you write it?

A. I don't recall. Wait. I do seem to recall a letter containing an allegation against Vincent.

Q. Do you recall what action you took?

A. I asked Vincent about it. He denied it. Told me they were a strange family.

Q. What did you do then?

A. Obviously I sent the parents this letter, but I don't recall writing it.

Q. You didn't believe the parents?
A. Over the word of a trusted associate? Hardly.

Q. Did you ever talk to the parents?
A. To what purpose?

Q. It is a rather serious matter.
A. (The cardinal shrugged his shoulders)

MR. GOULDING: For the record, this is a letter written above Cardinal O'Connell's signature apparently in response to Mr. Roelly's appeal for help. The letter questions the Roellys' integrity and denies the allegation out of hand. I have more questions, but it's time for a break. Fifteen minutes?

MR. PILASTER: Sounds good.

VIDEO OPERATOR: The time is 10:20 a.m. We will go off the record and stop the video.

VIDEO OPERATOR: The time is 10:36. We are back on the record.

Q. Your Eminence. Did you ever vacation with the three bishops: Barieno, Sandes, and Courteer?
A. Yes, I did.

Q. In this country?
A. Yes.

Q. In any foreign country?
A. I recall a trip to Brazil.

Q. How often did you vacation with them in Brazil?
A. I don't recall exactly.

Q. Several times?
A. Perhaps.

Q. Where in Brazil?

A. Rio de Janeiro.

Q. In the city? On the beach?

A. If I remember correctly, we were close to a beach. They enjoyed swimming.

Q. How did they address you while you were on vacation?

A. I permitted them to call me by my nickname.

Q. Which is?

A. Paddy. After my middle name Patrick.

Q. Did you permit them to call you Paddy at the chancery office?

A. No, never.

Q. When you were in Brazil with them, did you ever do business with a man who called himself Tonio Solo?

A. I . . . I can't say I recall that name.

Q. You appeared to be startled when I mentioned Tonio's name. Are you sure you can't remember?

A. Quite sure.

Q. I have here for your examination a deposition of Tonio Solo. It is as yet an unnumbered exhibit. You will see on page six he testifies that he provided sexual partners to you and to Barieno. He says there that your preference was young adult females. Is that true?

MR. PILASTER: Objection. You don't have to answer that question.

A. I'll answer it. It is not true.

Q. You did not refer to those sexual partners as "my girl from Ipanema?"

A. Absolutely not. That whole idea is libelous, pure and simple.

Q. You are under oath. You realize that?

A. Of course I do.

Q. On page eight, Tonio Solo testifies that he provided preadolescent boys to Vincent Barieno for sexual pleasure. Is that true?

A. It is not true. It is libelous.

Q. How can you be certain of Barieno's behavior there? Were you with him all hours?

A. I know the man! He is not a pedophile! Period! I can't make it any more clear than that.

MR. GOULDING: Thank you for your time, Your Eminence. No further Questions.

MR. KOBS: As you know, Your Eminence, I am the defense attorney for those three bishops. May I ask if you intend to remain in the city for a time, or will you be returning to your home in Arizona?

CARDINAL O'CONNELL: I have a small apartment here in the city. I intend to remain here through the trial. If I can be of assistance to you, please let me know. I will give you my phone number and address after we conclude here.

MR. GOULDING: If there are no further questions, this deposition is concluded. Once again, I thank you, Your Eminence, for permitting us to question you.

VIDEO RECORDER: The time is 11:26 a.m. The deposition is completed.

After the others had departed, Kobs looked at Goulding. "He'll make a terrific witness for you, Bill. I hope you'll put him on the stand."

"And open the way for you to cloud the issues. That stupid I'm not. You're welcome to put him on as a defense witness. I'm sure he'll tell the world what wonderful guys they are. The Roelly allegation against Barieno is another matter, and perhaps another trial."

"That boy was nearly eighteen when he killed himself. Doesn't the statute of limitations exclude a trial? Wait. Let me answer that myself. Barieno has been out of the state in Palm Sands. His years there don't count. Still, that trial wouldn't be in your jurisdiction, and I'm not hired as defense attorney on that charge."

"I've been talking to the D.A.'s office. They're onto it. See you back at the trial, Jim."

CATHERINE

It was like old times, the better times. Catherine, the cardinal's house-keeper, set a tray of hot hors d'oeuvres on an already laden cocktail table, then silently left the room. The four men sat in semicircular formation around the table. In plush chairs they angled both toward the table and toward an unlit fireplace. O'Connell used the apartment less frequently now. A few weeks here in late spring and again in early autumn were enough for the old man. He preferred the dry climate of Arizona, even the summer heat there.

Glasses tinkled with the sound of ice cubes, but the trial weighted their moods and revealed itself in feeble attempts at humor.

"You're looking good, Paddy," Barieno said, raising his glass.

"And you're still a smooth talking liar, Vinny." Age had dwindled Paddy's once robust laugh to a wheezing cackle.

"How did the deposition go today?" Sandes asked.

"They know about Ipanema. They got to Tonio."

"Oh, God, what next?" Barieno exclaimed.

"I don't think it's a problem," Paddy said. "Think about it. Knowing it and proving it are two very different things. They caught me by surprise today and I probably showed it, but I recovered as quickly as I used to. I've still got some muscle up here," he said, jabbing his index finger toward his skull. "Who'd take the word of a pimp over that of four bishops?" The cardinal's sharp eyes glinted at each of the others. "A good attorney would shred that testimony and taint all other testimony by doing so. Vatican politics taught me that. I'd bet anything you won't hear another word on Ipanema from the prosecutor during your trial. I denied everything at the deposition today."

"You said a 'good attorney.' We're not sure we've got a good attorney," Sandes said. "He wants us to change our plea to innocent by reason of mental defect. Says he can't defend a plain not guilty plea."

"Kobs is as good as they come, probably the best," Paddy replied. "I had him checked out as soon as I heard you hired him. Mental defect, eh? Well, that says he has imagination — and a sense of humor." Paddy's cackling led into a fit of coughing. "Catherine?" he stammered.

Alarmed, Barieno shouted, "Catherine."

She came running.

"Nitro," Paddy gasped.

Catherine had the bottle already in hand. She put one of the tiny pills into his mouth.

"Under your tongue with it," she said soothingly." She stayed until he recovered, then left quietly, her concern visible.

"Damn ticker," Paddy whispered hoarsely.

✠

Chapter Ten

PRIEST ABUSER

The priest was now serving a life sentence in a Texas prison. He had been assigned by Bishop Courteer as dean of a boarding school for underprivileged and homeless children. Known for the quality of its teaching staff, the school became a well-publicized endorsement of Bishop Courteer's policies.

Behind the scenes, a reign of sexual abuse of children went on relentlessly for several years by the dean and an assortment of housekeeping and teaching staff. Runaways, caught by the police, testified to the prevalence of abuse. They all alleged abuse done on them, both boys and girls.

Unable at first to prove conclusively the existence of abuse, the police brought the allegations to Bishop Courteer for his assistance. Courteer rejected the allegations outright, alleging that the children at the school were all street-wise and capable of any sort of blackmail. They were simply running from a discipline they had never before encountered. That discipline was necessary for them and they would emerge from it as useful, morally upright citizens.

The police brought the priest dean in for questioning. He denied all allegations. Those kids would say anything to cover their desire to evade discipline.

One by one, the police brought accused staff members in for

questioning. Eventually, with the D.A.'s cooperation and promises of immunity, they obtained confessions from a teacher and from the managing cook. Their testimony and that of the children was sufficient to convict the dean, two other teachers, and the head of housekeeping.

During that trial, evidence was introduced that many prior credible allegations of sexual abuse of children at the school had been brought to Courteer. Goulding questioned one of the witnesses on this point.

"Mrs. Maloney, did you personally give Bishop Courteer believable evidence supporting these allegations?"

"Yes, sir, I did."

"Where were you when you did this?"

"In the bishop's office at the chancery."

"Were you alone with the bishop?"

"No. Two other adults were with me."

"Their names, please?"

"Mr. James McNally and Mrs. Jane Simpson."

"What are their occupations?"

"They are certified psychotherapists like myself."

"How credible were these allegations?"

"In our minds, totally credible."

"On what did you base this credibility?"

"The abused children were ages seven to nine. They were completely innocent children. By that I mean they had no formal knowledge or experience of what sex or sexuality is about. They could only tell us what had been done to them graphically, pointing to parts of their bodies. They had no knowledge of its meaning, only that it left them with bad feelings."

"How did Bishop Courteer respond to these allegations?"

"He seemed to accept them. He thanked us profusely and said he would deal with the priest immediately. He did ask us to keep it all confidential for the children's sake."

"Did you do that?"

"I'm sorry to say we did. We trusted him."

"You didn't go to the police?"

"No, not then. We did when we heard of the boarding school incidents and trial."

"You have no doubt that Bishop Courteer knew of this priest's sexual abuse activities prior to assigning him to the boarding school?"

"None whatsoever."

"Thank you, Mrs. Maloney. Your witness Attorney Kobs."

BISHOP COURTEER

Scripture scholars say the Bible is not always factual, but it is always true. The prosecution's evidence of my actions may be factual, but it does not portray the whole truth. If this prosecution were about truth, it would have been built on Christ. "I am the way, the truth, and the life," Jesus said. He also said, "When the Spirit of truth comes, he will guide you into all the truth."

I have been through this rigorous logic almost daily. Jesus is the truth. The Holy Spirit has led the pope and bishops from the time of Jesus, guiding our thought, preventing us from error. Down through the centuries we have incorporated the truth of Christ into creeds, classic doctrinal formulas, and into our laws. Throughout my entire priestly career I have spent hours every day in study. If Goulding could only see my extensive library and my collection of rare books and manuscripts, he might put this scandal in perspective. I wish I could be in my library at this moment.

When some of my priests strayed from the truth, I didn't hesitate. When they openly supported homosexuality, I removed them from teaching and preaching positions. When they openly supported contraception, I gave them a choice. Obey and stay, or get out. Whatever the cost, even if the faithful were denied the sacraments for want of priests, I would not tolerate deviance from papal teaching by my subordinates. Truth runs a straight line. Any deviation is dangerous and unacceptable. When some priests and lay teachers wandered from the classical formulas with their "we must make truth meaningful to modern life experience," I would have none of it, and commanded their allegiance to the tried and true. Once, when they even told me "we should admit our mistakes," I demanded they show me a mistake. They revealed only their own deviations, and I fired them or placed them where they could do no harm.

When I discovered so-called reform organizations like Call to Action active in my diocese, I excommunicated their membership without hesitation. They seek reform, they say, but they extol the unacceptable and are not qualified. They lack the competence of episcopal authority. To protect the truth I now require that any person invited to speak on any diocesan property be vetted by me personally for their allegiance to orthodox Catholic teaching.

Lillith, bless my sister for her quaint charm, opposes me from time to time.

"Do you think the Holy Spirit is operative in the lives of everyday people?" she asked at an evening meal.

"Of course, I do." I said. "Operative for the conduct of their ordinary lives, but definitely not as formulators of truth. That role belongs to the hierarchy."

"They are without wisdom that might be helpful if considered?" she persisted.

"Considered perhaps, but only as consultative, not authoritative. The faithful must submit their wills and their intellects to proper authority in matters of faith and morals."

"So, truth comes down through a hierarchical funnel?"

"Something like that." I could sense her dander rise.

"In other words, to err is human, but not for combined papal/episcopal utterances?"

At that point my own ire began to rise. I simply shook my head, dismissing her question. "I'm very human, Lillith."

"Really? I have heard you preach on truth, on belief, and on obedience. If you have ever used the word compassion, Robert, it has only been in passing, another abstract thought. Summed up, your homilies promise that belief and obedience put people in the salvation safety net. I suggest that is pablum, Robert. Pablum for adults. You don't ask people to be compassionate. You only ask them to memorize."

"To teach the truth, the core beliefs, and to establish laws for the sake of order is both teaching compassion and being compassionate, Lillith."

"No. The only way to teach compassion is to be compassionate, Robert. Your Latin is better than mine, but I understand the root meaning of compassion is to suffer *with,* to feel *with.* Do you suffer with your people, Robert? Do you feel the pain of parents trying to express their love by being celibate? Do you suffer with AIDS patients who could be whole if they had used your prohibited contraception? Do you suffer with children abused by adults physically and sexually? Some of your priests are alleged abusers."

"How do you know that?"

"It's out there on the streets, Robert. I can't help but hear it. Parents tell parents. Parents warn parents. It gets around even when it doesn't make the newspapers."

"My first concern is for my priests, Lillith. I feel for them. I want the truth of their sinfulness to straighten out their lives. I protect them because I suffer from the damage they do to truth. People see priests as pillars of truth. Priests' sins throw truth into question, the church into question, Jesus into question. I protect them to protect all that."

"Can't you throw them out to protect your truth?"

"Part of our truth is forgiveness, Lillith. We do not punish sinners. We forgive. My decisions are not always easy."

"What about the abused children?"

"God will protect them. 'Let the children come to me,' Jesus said; 'Do not hinder them. The kingdom of God belongs to such as these.'"

"Can you feel what these abused little children feel, Robert?"

It was as if I suddenly had two sets of eyes. I stared at Lillith while staring inside myself. What did I feel? I could not feel their feelings. I knew of several suicides by abused children, but the cause was a mystery to me. Such a dire action for a moment's injustice? She was right. I live in my head and relate to abstractions. Am I unable to be compassionate? In conquering the thrust of sexuality, did I also root out the ability to feel? Lillith feels. What do I feel?

LILITH

I hate to see you up there, Robert. You're my brother and I love you. I pray for you every day. I've been at your side since you were assigned your first parish. I was so proud when you were elevated to bishop. To think that a Courteer from the other side of the tracks could rise so high. Now I've listened to the prosecutor apparently convict two of your fellow bishops for protecting pedophiles. It's your turn for his attention. I'm afraid. Dear God, I'm afraid for Robert. Help him.

I try to understand where you're coming from on these sexual things. All I've got to go on is that one time. I was twenty. You were eighteen, a seminarian home for the summer. Your words, how you pressed your case, remain with me as if it were yesterday.

"Lilith," you said, "I need to know what a woman's body is like in the flesh, not just what I imagine through clothing. It's important to me. I think it's important for my mission in life. When Mom and Dad are gone sometime, would you let me, you know, examine you? Touch you? Can we get naked together?"

"I'm your sister, Robert."

"I know that, but isn't that the way it should be? Shouldn't brothers and sisters be the first ones to help each other know about sex? Who else would do it?"

"It's not right, Robert."

"It is right, Lilith!"

You were so persistent. Day after day. I finally gave in. I can still feel you soaping my body in the shower. When we were dried you asked me to stand while you checked my body. I remember you gave me what I thought then was a hug. On the bed you kissed my lips ever so lightly. You moved your fingers over and around my breasts. You examined my vagina with your eyes and your fingers.

I'm getting some of the feeling back as I remember that scene. I was warm and moist, even ready for more. You abruptly got out of bed and stood there naked, your member as limp as when we started.

"Thank you, Lilith," you said, and walked out.

"I don't understand you, Robert. Maybe I don't understand sex."

BEN BAUER

Ben was rushing when he arrived at his parish office. He had helped Celina and Jeanne scrub the shelter's floor and kitchen area after breakfast hours. It had been a down-on-your-knees job. His trousers were wet and dirty, and he needed a shave. That could wait until after the staff meeting.

"They want you down at the chancery, Ben. Pronto." Margie

Dunleavy, parish director of adult education, was waiting inside the door. "I've cancelled the staff meeting. If it's okay, I'll check your calendar and reschedule."

"Thanks, Margie. Did they say what it's about?"

"No."

"Who called?"

"He didn't say. Just that the cardinal wanted you there *now*."

"Can't be good news," Ben said.

"Pessimist," she teased.

"Mind the store, Margie. I'll change clothes and get down there. And, just for you, I won't entertain negative speculations. We'll know soon enough."

He entered the chancery at nine fifty-five a.m.

"The receptionist informed him that the cardinal had just left the office. "It shouldn't be long, Father. A haircut, I think he said."

Ben went to a restroom adjacent to the lobby. He checked himself in the mirror. His hurried shave had left a few missed spots. It'll do, he thought. Thank God for light-colored hair. He examined himself. Your forty-six years are starting to show, my friend. There's gray starting at the temples.

He returned to the reception area and took a seat. His attention drifted to a large portrait on the wall in front of him. The reigning cardinal, staff in hand and mitre on head, beamed smugly at the viewers. At fifty-six the prelate was young for the office. His full head of black hair was barely tinted by gray. The skin tone of his face was almost baby-like. Ben checked the reading material on the table next to his seat. Pamphlets. He scanned a few of them. Pablum, he thought and turned his attention to structuring a homily for the coming Sunday.

At eleven he checked again with the receptionist. Had the cardinal been unexpectedly detained? She had no word on that.

Homily in mind, he went back to the receptionist at noon.

"I simply don't have a clue," she told him.

"I'm going out for a sandwich," He told her. "I presume the cardinal eats lunch." He was back at twelve thirty.

At one thirty the cardinal arrived at the office, walked through the reception area where Ben sat, but gave Ben no acknowledgment.

A clue, Ben thought. It's time for a bit of pessimism. I'm being reminded of my humble status. He suppressed a smile. I'm okay with that, the status I mean.

At two fifteen the receptionist called over. "His Eminence will see you now, Father. His office is down that hall, last door on the right."

Corner office with a lake view. Ben had been there a few times. He walked to the office, entered, and stood by the door.

The cardinal was reading something, his head down. After several minutes he looked at Ben. "Have a seat, Father Bauer," he said, pointing to one across the desk from him.

"Thank you," Ben said and took the seat.

The cardinal continued a perusal of a stack of papers for several more minutes. Then he put the stack down and looked at Ben. "So—" he said.

"So?" Ben replied. He felt at ease, above the humiliation zone.

"So, what's this I hear about you, Father Bauer?" His neck stretched up, his head tilted back, giving the appearance that he looked down on Ben.

"That I'm a hard worker, a good homilist, and very funny?" Ben asked.

"Not funny, Father Bauer. What I hear is definitely not funny."

"I imagine you're going to tell me what you heard, Cardinal, so I can respond to it." He kept within himself, not defensive. No games for me, he thought.

"It has come to my attention that you secretly permitted a meeting of the so-called Women's Ordination Conference to be held in your parish facilities."

"It was certainly not secret," Ben replied. "The meeting was announced in the parish bulletin, and advertised in several local newspapers."

"So you admit such a meeting was held?"

"Of course. I attended the meeting."

"Did they conduct a prayer service?"

"Yes. Very nice."

"Did a woman preside at that service?"

"Yes. And she led the discussion."

"Did she wear a stole?"

"Now that you mention it, I think she did."

"You endorsed that meeting by your presence, Father Bauer. I can't believe it."

"I attended it."

"And did they discuss women's ordination?"

"Of course they did. That's their main shtick."

"You are not aware that the pope has forbidden all discussion of that topic?"

"I'm aware of it. It's silly, really. The people are going to talk about it, pope or no pope."

"Silly? You're over the line, Father Bauer."

"I don't think so, Cardinal. I think it's the other way around. Nearly eighty percent of our people think the pope is 'over the line' on the issue of birth control; almost seventy percent on women's ordination. If the pope thinks he's going to suppress discussion of these issues by fiat, he's totally out of touch. Isn't it your job to keep him in touch with what the people think?"

"I don't need you to tell me my job, Father Bauer."

"Wouldn't it be a good idea to get all the priests together and discuss these issues?" Ben asked.

"There is nothing to discuss. *Roma locuta est, causa finita est.* Have you heard that before, Father Bauer?"

"*Rome has spoken, the matter is finished.* Sure, I know that old cliché. And that's silly too. Are we so afraid to discuss issues that we have to shut them down with a hammer? Is that honest?"

"Are you saying I'm dishonest?" His eyes widened.

"I'm saying we should talk about the things the people are going to talk about whether we want them to or not. We should be part of the discussion."

"You've forgotten that we tell the people what they are to think on matters of faith and morals. You are aware, Father Bauer, that you are bound by a promise of obedience to me, your cardinal?"

"Of course."

"Under that promise I am directing you never to permit discussions on parish property on any issue already decided by His Holiness."

"I can't promise that."

"I beg your pardon?"

"Obedience does not call for me to violate my own conscience. I can't promise what you're asking."

The cardinal stared at Ben, his face flushed with anger. "Permit me to remind you of a few things, Father Bauer. I can remove you from your parish at anytime. I can put you on the street. I can take away any and all benefits, health insurance, retirement benefits — all of them. And I assure you, I am capable of doing it all. Before you leave today you will sign a letter I've had prepared where you admit your mistake for permitting that meeting and disavowing its purpose. In it you will avow complete submission to the papal position on this issue. That letter will be printed in our diocesan newspaper."

"I won't sign that letter, Cardinal."

"We will print it anyway. Now get out of here. I will decide your fate later."

On his way out Ben couldn't resist. "You have a nice day, Cardinal."

At the shelter that night Ben described the meeting to Jim Kobs. "That's the purple style, Jim. Put one or two of the dissidents down and scare the hell out of the rest. They don't dare put all of us down, so they won't meet with all of us on the real issues."

Chapter Eleven

CATHERINE

This is so boring. Witness after witness. Question after question. How could anybody keep up with it all? Paddy should be back in the warmth of Arizona, but he insists on being here. "I stand by my friends," he said. If the truth be told, sometimes he can barely stand. I couldn't let him come alone. What if he had an attack here? Who would help him? He's so helpless that way. Did I bring the nitro? Yes. It's here in my purse.

At least we sit together now that he's old and no longer frets about giving scandal. It's hard to believe so many years have passed. I was only twenty-six. It seems like only yesterday that he interviewed me to be his personal secretary. I remember how scared I was. I'd never been that close to a bishop before.

My work experience wasn't all that great, just a couple of clerk-type jobs. I had been an average student and I was perhaps a bit below-average typist. But I knew a little shorthand. He told me not to worry. My skills would pick up, and besides, he was more interested in how our personalities blended. I remember thinking his concern was so sweet.

I could scarcely believe it when he hired me. The salary wasn't that great. He sort of apologized for that and said the church ran on a low budget so more could go to the poor. It's funny that I never put two and two together when I finally came to know the cost of his personal maintenance. I should have asked for a bigger salary right then. I guess I was afraid. What if he became angry with me?

Still, I was thrilled to be working for him. I think I stood in awe of him for years. He was so important. And he was so handsome, chiseled face like a Greek god, wavy black hair. Oh my!

He didn't keep me all that busy, but after about six months he began to pressure me to move into the bishop's mansion. "There's a vacant apartment there," he told me. "It's very nice, and we won't charge you rent. You'll be available to help me when I need you."

I was torn. I had met a really nice man about then. We dated and seemed to be growing closer. When I told that to the bishop, he wanted to know the man's name, what he did, where he worked, how much he made, just all kinds of things."

He kept pressuring me for months to move in. He said he couldn't afford to hire a second secretary, one for the office and one for the mansion. About that time my boyfriend told me his company was transferring him to Japan. He didn't invite me to go with him, just said he'd write and that he'd only be gone two years. We'd pick up where we left off when he got back. I never heard from him again.

I finally gave in to the bishop and moved into the mansion. The apartment was lovely indeed, and on the same floor as his private rooms. He soon had me acting as both secretary and hostess for his many entertainments. I was scared at first, being around all those important people. But he affirmed me and gave me confidence. It wasn't long before I felt comfortable talking to those people, calling them to arrange appointments and parties. Eventually he left it to me to plan menus, arrange for entertainment, and so forth. I even learned to like wine and how to choose the better vintages for his cellar.

It was about a year and a half after he employed me that he began to pressure me for a more intimate relationship. He told me I would be serving God by serving God's bishop. "A man can't live and do his best without a woman's help," he said. "Catherine, I need you," he said. "Catherine, you need a man," he said. "We can be complete partners," he said. "Silent partners," he said.

Several months after he began pressuring me, I gave in. By then I knew that I loved him. I think I was afraid he'd fire me and I'd lose him. It was difficult at times, but I've never regretted it. A man does need a woman. Paddy needed me. He needs me more than ever now that he's old.

When he became an archbishop, he moved us here to the archdiocese. The mansion here is so much bigger. He put me in charge of the cleaning persons and the cook. He was sixty then. I was thirty-four. Our relationship was still warm and still physical. He no longer housed me on the same floor. His quarters took up the entire second floor. I had an apartment on the third. "Lest we give scandal," he said. I would go to his apartment when he called.

He was made a cardinal shortly after that. The splendor around him increased. I began to feel a bit more like a servant than a partner. Always in the background. Always serving him and those he entertained, never an equal, not even in bed.

The witness had testified to the foreknowledge Courteer had of yet another pedophile priest's abusive activities. Goulding concluded his questioning.

"Thank you, Mrs. Duggan. No further questions, Your Honor."

"Your witness, Mr. Kobs," Judge Monroe said.

"No questions, Your Honor."

"Mr Goulding?"

"The prosecution rests its case, Your Honor."

Judge Monroe turned to Kobs. "You may proceed with the defense, Mr. Kobs."

Kobs reached for some papers and stood. "We have a change of plea motion to make first, Your Honor. May we approach the bench?"

"You may."

Kobs delivered a copy of the motion to the judge and then a copy to Bill Goulding.

Judge Monroe scanned the motion quickly. "Mr. Kobs, Mr. Goulding, kindly meet me in my chambers. Ladies and gentlemen of the jury. It is now eleven ten a.m. We will recess until two this afternoon."

In her chambers, the judge's stern eyes were fixed on Kobs. "An insanity plea, Mr. Kobs? At this late date?"

"It's a typical Kobs ploy, Your Honor," Goulding said, his exasperation clearly visible. "Mr. Kobs wants to delay the trial, hoping time will distance the jury from the hard evidence. It's an obfuscation ploy, pure and simple. He should not be permitted to get away with it."

Kobs was apologetic. "I realize this late change of plea is unusual, Your Honor, and I understand Mr. Goulding's rush to judgment as to my motive. Permit me to explain. From the time I took on the defense of these bishops, I have been troubled by my inability to find a motive for their tragic lack of appropriate behavior."

The raised eyes of the judge revealed her skepticism. "Did you ask them?"

"In my own way I did, Your Honor. Their responses were of no help. They thought I couldn't possibly understand the role of a bishop. And they were unable to explain beyond that enigmatic statement. I set out on my own, beginning with only a few trail signs given me by a priest friend. I followed that trail through an array of experts. It has taken me all these months to arrive at the conclusion that is reflected in the changed plea. I might add that the bishops are unhappy with this change, but I was able to persuade them of this plea's legitimacy."

"Your Honor, this is pure baloney," Goulding interjected.

Kobs turned to Goulding. "You tell us, Bill. Did their actions or inaction flow from ignorance or from evil?"

"Either way the law puts them in jail," Goulding responded.

"Mr. Goulding, you did not answer the question," the judge said.

"I admit I don't fully understand their motive, Your Honor. They're guilty! Period! And they're not crazy!"

"Your Honor, don't the defendants have the right to have a jury make that determination?" Kobs asked.

Judge Monroe sat quietly for a few minutes, her fingers smoothing the folds in her judicial garb, her eyes downcast. "Gentlemen," she said lifting her head, " you have both argued cases in my court before. I respect you both. It is a pleasure to witness the competence you bring to the practice of law."

"Thank you," Goulding responded.

"In this instance, I'm ruling in favor of the motion. If you are correct, Mr. Kobs, you have formidable obstacles to overcome. And Mr. Goulding, you will have the opportunity to prove this plea to be disguised baloney. Mr. Kobs, do you have a list of the experts you intend to call?"

"I do, Your Honor." Kobs extracted two copies of the list from a briefcase and handed one to the judge, and one to Goulding."

"Mr. Goulding," the judge said, "I presume you will want your own experts to examine the defendant's sanity?"

"Of course."

"Will four weeks time be sufficient?"

"Yes."

"Very good. When we reconvene this afternoon, I will instruct the jury on this change of plea and recess the trial for one month. Mr. Goulding, when we reconvene, you will continue the prosecution's case with your witnesses." Turning to Kobs, "Then it will be your turn, Mr. Kobs."

"Thank you," Kobs replied.

JACOB

I live in a different world today. It has all changed. My spirit feels lighter, like I'm floating, feet coasting along above the ground. She sliced the knot, she brought the prison walls down, she made the sunlight brighter and the colors more vivid. Inez did it. She could talk a fox out of its den.

She looked at me and held my eyes there in our family room last night.

"You were abused as a child, weren't you, Jacob?" she said. "I know your family was Catholic once. It was a priest, wasn't it? That's why you're going to that trial every day?"

Numb, I stared at her. When I finally nodded, my whole body started to shake. I felt fragmented, a dam breaking up under too much pressure. At first I thought it was my heart giving out some last bursts of energy. The tears started to flow and my sobbing took on the tempo of my shaking body. Inez came and sat on the arm of my chair and pulled my head to her breasts. By the time I recovered some control, the front of her blouse was wet.

"Jacob, Jacob, why didn't you tell me? All these years?"

"I didn't know how," I said.

"You're a strong man, Jacob, sometimes too strong for your own good. It would have made no difference. It makes no difference now. You're my Jacob and I love you."

Right there and then she decided to come to the rest of this trial with me. She's next to me and already has that pretty young girl in conversation. If that girl is a fox hiding in its den, she won't be in that den very long. Inez will have her story before the girl knows she's telling it. I can remember how, at office parties, I'd come home trying to remember who was there. Inez would bring all their histories back with her.

I don't mind sitting here even if the judge did recess until two this afternoon. We've plenty of time to get lunch. It's nice to sit here when the courtroom isn't buzzing with questions. And I don't want to disturb Inez's conversation.

So, we're taking Deenah to lunch Inez tells me. That's my wife! I didn't even know the girl's name was Deenah, and I've been sitting next to her all these days. The trial would be over and I probably still wouldn't know her name. Inez introduces me.

"Pleased to meet you, Deenah. Call me Jacob. It'll make me feel younger."

Deenah smiles a timid smile.

At the restaurant I'm thinking the bacon, liver, and onion special, but I know that freedom is gone. Inez orders for me: cottage cheese, fruit, turkey on whole wheat, mustard instead of mayo.

I munch on the sandwich and listen to the information exchange. Inez gets a hundred bytes of data for every ten Deenah gets. Deenah is waitressing at night and going to the trial by day. She lives in a rented room in one of the old former mansions downtown. She intends to get a full-time day job after the trial. Wants to save for college. Parents can't help. They've moved to Atlanta. I get the feeling that the parent relationship is strained. They don't communicate much. No siblings. She was a good student in high school, A-minus grade point average. Says she didn't work as hard as she could have.

The info comes out at Inez's unobtrusive questioning, mixed with bytes about the trial and about us, the Jacob Briands. Isn't that Goulding good looking? Kobs just sits there. The bishops are guilty. How could they be so stupid and cruel? The Jacob Briands never had children, a deep regret. Jacob was a successful engineer, had his own engineering firm. Inez was a kindergarten teacher for thirty years. Loved it! Loves children. The Briands are comfortable. Deenah must come and see our place. It's spacious.

I don't see it coming. Can hardly believe my ears when Inez says in her confidential voice:

"Deenah, why are you going to the trial? Were you abused by a priest *like Jacob was?*"

I am astounded at this breach of confidence. How could she? I look at Inez, and read her eyes. She wants to give Deenah an opening and an understanding companion for her journey.

Deenah looks at me, then avoids my eyes and nods. Tears begin to seep out.

Inez reaches for one hand. I reach for the other. We both say, "It's okay."

I say, "Deenah, there is life after abuse, trust me." I have tears in my eyes too. So does Inez. We sit there holding hands.

Later, when the judge announces a month recess, Inez makes a date for lunch with Deenah for tomorrow. I know Inez. We're going to have a weekend guest.

FABIAN

"Where's the conspiracy?" Helen was yelling! I held the phone six inches off my ear while she ran her standard list of enemies, the core Catholic haters: "Secular humanists," she shouts, "the rainbow sash, stinking cafeteria Catholic relativists, ex-priests—"

"Helen, there is no conspiracy," I said, my mind recalling all the reporters she has discarded. I was depending on Ralph's skills, the ones that go beyond his editorial post, to save my butt. I've been with *True Catholic* for thirty-two years. Great editors, narrow owner. She still hauls out the same yellowed pages for every speech she gives, adapting it only to the issue at hand.

"If I were the jury, I'd send these three bishops to prison. I can say that without hearing the defense," I told her. "They're guilty. The defense attorney will use an insanity defense. That's all he's got. However it goes down in the end, these guys are losers. Don't keep backing them. Cut them loose and save *True Catholic* some embarrassment. At least take the story off the front page. You should accept the fact we've got bad bishops, just like we've had bad popes in the past."

She grumbled a few comments about lazy, incompetent reporters and hung up. That's okay. As long as I'm around, I'll tell it the way I see it.

I keep asking myself, how did guys like these get into the episcopacy? I think the Second Vatican Council set it up. These three are just one sample of the unintended consequences of the council. At the root of it, obedience suffered under the council's emphasis on personal liberty and freedom of conscience. When obedience suffers, authority suffers. These guys, like others, forgot their job is to exercise authority. They were too tolerant, too much into forgiveness and second chances. They should have chopped the legs off those abusers at the first instance.

Maybe that's the key to all this. At least it's good enough for the summation I'll call in at five. God gave bishops authority. That authority doesn't come from people. Bishops are meant to exercise authority. People are called to obey. It's that simple. If your conscience is out of line with what the bishops say, you're the one with the problem.

I can't understand why liberals don't see that. If you join a church, you go by its rules. If you don't buy into those rules or the authority behind them, you leave — if you're honest. You can't be both a draft dodger and soldier. If you want to be a dodger, go to Canada.

All these priests and nuns who deserted their ministries but continue to proclaim their personal issues — married priests, women priests, whatever — should shut up. They walked away, afraid to speak their issues while they were on the job. Who can respect that? The way I see it, anyone who puts their own personal interpretation on morals or dogma, counter to the official teaching of the church magisterium, must be arrogant beyond measure. Where are you when you leave that safety net? A wanderer in the limitless space of your own ego, that's where.

RENEE

I'm not sure how much my theology degree and teaching experience qualify me to judge here, but this change of plea is intriguing. The defense clearly sees the change as their sole remaining option. I'd vote guilty right now, but I'm not sure about insanity. My experience with bishops tells me they're guilty, not from malicious evil intent, but from ignorance and naïveté. As a group, bishops aren't known for superior intellectual skills. They get promoted for unrelenting loyalty to Rome, and all that loyalty entails, like repressing thought perceived by them as a threat to the institutional structure.

It's curious. The hierarchy has permitted all sorts of superstitious alloys to meld with their idea of the "true faith." Voodoo is excused because the participants are considered ignorant. When the bishops revoke the teaching licenses of theologians who look for new ways of understanding and expression, who is ignorant?

They are inconsistent with their exclusions. They won't excommunicate the 80 percent of the laity who, having experienced that service to life can coexist with a condom, shed official teaching on contraception. They won't impose excommunication or interdict on those in power who refuse to put an end to starvation, AIDS, and slavery in the world today. I suspect that goes with a follow-the-money mentality. They would lose many wealthy benefactors if they ever dared put force behind social responsibilities. They won't listen to the wisdom of the laity, so who is ignorant?

Why is a mix of voodoo okay, but serious intellectual search isn't? There is more evidence in the gospels for the full equality of women than there is for a monarchical hierarchy. Yet women are to know their place, that is, the place where bishops would place them. So who is ignorant?

They are men who rely on authority and a strict demand for obedience while never having to prove competence. I see obedience as an overrated virtue, all too often called on to hide the bishops' lack of competence. So who is ignorant?

If you need a reason why these three bishops ignored victims and protected abusers, I'd go with ignorance.

Whatever! I can bring Ben up to date on the trial this evening. He's interested, but can't spare the time to come. He told me that both Goulding and Kobs are his friends. I wonder if they know how lucky they are. I wonder if they appreciate the depth that Ben brings to any issue. Ben is not ignorant.

Chapter Twelve

DEENAH

Lace around the sheets? I've never slept in a bed this fancy. It's at least twice the size that Father Dan's was, and the room is at least five times the size of mine at the rooming house. Mine would fit into this room's bathroom. I was nervous coming here, but that feeling went away fast. They're such nice people. They make me feel so welcome.

I never knew my grandparents. They all died before I was born. When I told Inez she was like the grandmother I never had, the words just slipped out. For a moment I thought I'd hurt her feelings. But her eyes lit up and she got this big smile.

"Thank you, Deenah," she said. "That is simply wonderful to hear. I like to think of you as my granddaughter."

I like Jacob too. He doesn't talk as much as Inez, but he's warm and caring. He gives me a hug every morning. And nobody ever opened a car door for me before, or helped me carry things. I think he likes me too. He says I'm easy to be around.

Inez took me to lunch four times over the past two weeks, and I've been staying at their house for three days now.

I've never been in Winnetka before. The homes are huge. The gardens are beautiful out my window. The creek along their back-yard just sort of meanders. Inez says the house is her responsibility, but the gardens are Jacob's. He spends a lot of time there. Yesterday I helped him plant.

I wish I could have been a kid here. I don't think about my parents very often since they moved away. My mother never writes. I wonder if she wants to forget that she sent me to Father Dan. I wonder if I want to forget them because they didn't help me. They don't seem to care. Maybe they don't know how to care.

It's hard for me to trust anybody. But it's hard not to trust Inez and Jacob. When I told them they do too much for me, Jacob said that life's pleasures get fewer as they get older. But, loving and helping is one pleasure they still have. I never heard anyone say that before. He made it sound like they get more than I do from our relationship.

"Stop being a victim, Deenah," my therapist told me. "Do something. Get mad. If you won't tell me the man's name, go tell the police. What he did to you is called statutory rape. It doesn't make any difference if you went along with it. What he did was illegal and immoral. Some people are like that guy," she said. "They get their sexual jollies only from a certain age group. Pedophiles go for children. Ephebophiles, like the priest who used you and then discarded you, go for adolescents. And when one of his victims gets older than he prefers, he ditches her and gets another girl. Now do something. Go to the police."

I couldn't go to the police. I was afraid. It would be my word against his. Who would believe me against the word of a priest? Last week that changed. Some friends of Inez told her about an organization called SNAP. It stands for Survivors Network of those Abused by Priests. She checked it out and we decided to attend a meeting. So many people, so many stories. They really help each other.

At the meeting I accidentally met the girl who replaced me with Father Dan. Her name is Susan. I got her in a conversation and asked her how things were going with her and Father Dan. I remember the startled look on her face.

"What do you mean?" she said, trying to cover up her surprise.

I don't know how I managed it, but I told her about Father Dan and me. "I was with him as his lover for three years," I said. "Then he ditched me."

She broke down and cried.

I felt sorry for her and put my arm around her shoulder.

"I'm so angry," she said. "He did the same to me. Now he's got another freshman in his clutches. He'll do the same thing to her. Get her in bed and string her along until the next one."

"I could never go alone to the police," I said. "But now it's not just my word against a priest. Now it's two of us." I told Inez about Susan on the way home. She fixed it so the three of us had lunch. There she told Susan and me that we should see an attorney. She and Jacob would pay the fee.

"Will you come with us?" I asked.

"Of course, if you both want that. So will Jacob if you ask him," she said.

We all went.

The attorney advised us to go to the police. He went with us. We told the police everything. They asked us things we never thought about telling, like where does Father Dan keep his condoms? Does he keep a diary? We could answer a lot of that kind of question.

Afterward, our attorney said that they'll probably set up a sting operation on Father Dan. He felt positive they'll get him. I hope they do. I'm ready to testify.

I think I'll get over this empty feeling if I can do something. Thanks to Inez and Jacob I now feel strong enough to stand up publicly and tell the truth. When Inez told Jacob about SNAP, he sat down and wrote them a check.

JACKSON

Lucy is on my back something fierce. "Get a job," she says. "I can't support both of us on my job, what with the mortgage and everything," she says. "You're gonna cost us all our retirement savings," she says. "You're not going to like a retirement diet of oatmeal," she says. "You were never lazy, Jackson," she says. "So get off your butt and go back to work." Lucy can be tough. Jumping Jesus, that's why I love her. She's like me, stubborn as a rock.

When we first got married, that's five years now, Lucy wasn't enthusiastic about church like I was, but she would go with me on Sunday. After a while she just stopped. She wouldn't talk about why. And I could never put no numbers around that one.

Me, I was brought up strict. I liked it. If Lucy and I ever get lucky and have kids, you can bet I'll be strict, too. I believe in spare the rod, spoil the child. That don't seem to fly with a lot of people these days, but it flies with me. My old man didn't spare the rod, and I came out real good. Ma was good with the switch too, when she had reason. I gave them both plenty of reason. And we went to church every Sunday. They made me go to confession every Saturday, just like they had to do when they were kids. I'm okay with all that. Wouldn't have it any other way. I wish I could figure out what's eating Lucy. It'd be nice if she went to church with me.

I can't give up this trial. I got this feeling God wants me there. He needs me to be there. I figure he wants me to tell Kobs how to do it. Geez, I shoulda been a lawyer myself.

I hope Kobs doesn't get too highbrow. He should keep it simple. Numbers are simple. I can't understand why those lawyers don't use numbers. I admit, this case is a tough one to put numbers around. I been trying, but so far nothing. I'm always a couple numbers off. That's okay once in a while, but not every time.

I'm gonna keep working on it, and I'll get it yet. So far I haven't started on dates, like what happened back through history on the date this trial started. That's next. Then I'll lay the facts on Kobs. I can tell he needs some help. Those priests they're talking about were framed. I'm sure of that. No priest of God is gonna abuse a kid or a woman. I figure those so-called victims are just after money. Church equals cash cow to them. And jumping Jesus these guys are bishops. God don't make crooks and nutsy guys a bishop. The Holy Spirit would see to that.

Maybe Kobs will split the fee with me. Jackson, you gotta save the day here. You can do it. Two more weeks and the trial starts again. When Lucy comes home, stay out of the way. Get out of the house. You can work the numbers and dates at the bar.

The witness spoke her qualifications in crisp order. Dressed in business attire she exhibited calm and competence.

Bill Goulding went directly to the point. "Dr. McDonald, in your professional judgment do these three defendants suffer from a mental defect sufficient to prevent them from knowing right from wrong?"

"They do not."

"They are sane by current psychiatric standards?"

"They are."

"Specifically, is Bishop Sandes sane, and does he know right from wrong?"

"He is, and he does."

"Is Bishop Courteer sane, and does he know right from wrong?"

"He is, and he does."

"Is Bishop Barieno sane, and does he know right from wrong?"

"He is, and he does."

"There is no question in your mind as to their sanity?"

"None."

"Thank you, Dr. McDonald." Goulding looked at Judge Monroe. "No further questions, Your Honor."

"Your witness, Mr. Kobs," Monroe said.

Kobs walked a bear-like amble to the witness stand. "Dr. McDonald," he asked, "would you take us through the process you followed in arriving at your finding of sanity."

"Certainly. Do you want me to go through the various questions and tests given them, or the various determinations I made in the process?"

"Let's begin with the determinations. That should be sufficient. If necessary I might ask for the specifics of any particular finding."

"May I use my notes?"

"You may."

"Very well. I first assessed whether each man was correctly oriented in all three spheres. They were."

"Sorry to stop you so soon. Would you name the spheres for the jury, please?"

"They refer to person, time, and place."

"Go on."

"I examined them for evidence of mood disorders that would interfere with cognitive functioning. I found none. I tested both their recent and their remote memory. Both were intact. I found their language functioning to be consistent with their educational level." She looked at Kobs. "Are these the types of determinations you want?"

Kobs smiled. "You're doing fine. Are there more?"

"Oh yes. I found their social judgment to be appropriate, and inferred adequate occupational functioning from contextual clues. They are capable of mathematical reasoning, and their judgment appears to be unimpaired. They are able to distinguish between external and internal reality."

"Explain that last one a bit more, please?"

"Do they know the difference between objective and subjective reality?"

"Thank you. Please continue."

"Their intelligence level extends from slightly below to slightly above average. My cognitive assessment indicated no impairment in executive functions, or in their understanding of categories, similarities, and differences. Their reaction times are appropriate for their ages. They do not exhibit either undue anxiety or hostility. They can appreciate humor, but are quicker to respond to humor with a religious theme. They admit to no delusions or hallucinations. Their perceptual organization of nonverbal concepts is within the average range. The personality factors they exhibit do not significantly affect their cognitive functioning. Finally, they understand court procedures, what is happening here, and are able to participate in them." Dr. McDonald looked at Kobs. "Is that sufficient?"

"Yes, it is. It is most helpful. Thank you. No further questions."

Chapter Thirteen

Kobs stood about three paces from the center of the jury box, his demeanor pleasant but serious. He took the time to look at each juror, catching their eyes if they permitted. Concerned at the beginning of the trial that his strategy might change along the way, he had reserved the defense's opening statement until now.

"Ladies and gentlemen of the jury," he began, "you have heard the testimony of a psychiatrist for the prosecution testify that Bishop Sandes, Bishop Courteer, and Bishop Barieno are sane, that they are without any psychological impediment or mental defect that might prevent moral and legal conformity.

He walked to the corner of the jury box. Their eyes followed him. He had their attention. "You should be aware of the power you have," he said. "You, and you alone, will make the determination as to whether these defendants suffer mental defect. You! Not the psychiatrists, not me, and not Prosecutor Goulding. You should also be aware that in matters of law, it has often been jurors who dared to break old boundaries and carried the law and justice to new and higher planes. Such is the power of a jury. Such is your power.

"I want to emphasize that we are speaking to the legal understanding of insanity. It is the inability to distinguish right from wrong at the time an offense is committed. You will come to see through the testimony of experts that this form of insanity can be found where factors such as psychosis and the usual run of psychotic illnesses are not found. It is not that I disagree with Dr. McDonald's assessment of the defendants, made as it was on the basis of current psychological practice.

Kobs walked to a large screen, positioned so that it was visible to judge, jury, and audience. David sat behind a projector. Marcie brought Kobs a pointer.

"I repeat, Dr. McDonald was absolutely consistent with the tenets of psychology when she declared these men to be sane, to be without mental defect. However, there exist specific cultural mores that fly beneath the screen of modern psychological discernment and do cause impairment of moral judgment. Please follow me as I will take you on the same intellectual journey I followed on the way to the conclusion that these men suffer from a mental defect. It is a defect of sufficient intensity to render them incapable of making the moral decisions they should have made in the cases brought before you. At the end of that journey the defense will rest. The decision will be in your competent hands."

David projected a bulleted list on the screen.

"Along the way of our investigation," Kobs began, "we will examine a series of cultures and subcultures. Experts will tell you that culture is simply the learned behavior that we take for granted as setting the standard of normalcy. That is why we experience culture shock when we are confronted with cultures that significantly differ from our own. Eating dog meat is not usual in our culture. Casting female babies out to die is not something acceptable in our culture. But they are or have been in other cultures. I believe you will agree at the end of our journey that the moral compass is misaligned in each of those cultures. Magnetic lodestones of various design have intruded, and have seduced the needle from the moral true North in each of them. Kobs began at the top, reciting the list without further detail:

> * The culture of royalty and aristocracy
> * The culture of addiction

* The culture of a cult
* The culture of narcissism
* The culture of power
* The culture of the episcopacy

In our closing statement, we will bring together all of the apparent unrelated cultures and show their convergence on the subject of this trial. You will, of course, be left to draw your own conclusions, the one that best explains the motive behind the behavior of these defendants. Thank you for your attention."

Judge Monroe announced the luncheon recess. Kobs left with the bishops. Marcie and David lingered by the defense table.

"Looking back, Marcie, did Jim's jury selection surprise you as much as it did me?"

"I've got it on my list to talk about when the trial is over," Marcie replied. "At the time I would not have challenged the ones he did, and I would have challenged the ones he didn't."

"Me too. But I think I'm beginning to see what he had in mind."

"He let all the brain power stay in the box. Is that what you mean?" Marcie asked.

"Right. The history Ph.D. The psychotherapist. The professionals. Usually they'd be gone on peremptory challenges," David said.

"So he was looking for jurors who can follow a convergence of data. No. Not data. This trial isn't about numbers. Concepts, a convergence of concepts."

"He did get rid of that CEO though. How does that fit?" David asked.

"Too much like bishops, maybe? Remember the guy who worked in a laundry. Jim asked if he'd finished high school. 'What for?' the guy answered. He was gone."

"Or the lady who said her husband gave her all the answers. And she wanted it that way. Gone."

CATHERINE

To think I nearly lost him only three days ago. The angina attack was powerful and debilitating. Yet, here he is. I don't know why he has to be at this trial. Any one of them, Vinny, Wilbur, or Bob, would bring him the news at the end of each day. They usually show up anyway. But no, he has to be here. I warn him, but he doesn't listen. I think this is entertainment for him. He chortles all the way home after each session. I'm sure he believes his boys are in no real jeopardy.

When he recovered from this last attack, I found the nerve to challenge him on his commitment to me. Years ago he promised he would take care of me when he died. "Don't worry, Catherine," he said more than once, "I'll see that you are provided for." I would be in his will, he said. But he never did anything about it. I've mentioned this to him several times over the past few years. "There's plenty of time, Catherine," he'd say. "My ticker has a billion or so more ticks in it. Don't worry. I'll get to it." He never did. He thinks he's immortal. Now he's promised to get it done as soon as we get back to Arizona. We'll see!

I don't want to appear money hungry, but the fact is, left to myself, I'd be impoverished. After all these years I have several thousand dollars saved. But what's that? Most of what I've earned went to satisfy his wishes. If he traveled and needed me along, I'd pay my own fare. When he wouldn't buy some medicines prescribed for him, I paid for them. He always wanted me to look nice, so I dressed well for him. And it cost all I had. I feel so poor. I am poor! After all these years I've finally turned some of my attention to myself, and that's what I see. Poverty! It's hard enough to think of life without him, but to think of life at my age — you're fifty-eight, Catherine — with no place to live and nothing to live on frightens me beyond words. I don't have the courage to peer into that sort of future. Please, God, take care of him — and me.

✠

The witness, an attractive brunette, faced Kobs from the stand. She recited an impressive array of credentials and, not yet fifty, stated she was a full professor in cultural anthropology at the university, and a consultant at a major museum. When finished, she flashed a bright smile at Kobs.

Kobs began his questioning:

"Your specialty goes to royal or absolutist cultures, does it not, Dr. Sheridan?"

"Yes, it does. Specifically it deals with royal cultures of the western world and Russia, though I have made some studies in Egyptian royal culture."

"How did absolute rulers come into being in the western world?"

"Objection, Your Honor," Goulding called out as he stood up. "This irrelevance goes beyond imagination. Attorney Kobs might just as well start his argument with the Big Bang."

"I promise I won't retreat to the Big Bang, Your Honor," Kobs said, smiling. "That is, unless Mr. Goulding insists we go back to atoms and quarks. This royal culture is relevant, however, and I will connect it to the matter at hand."

"Overruled," Judge Monroe pronounced. "Proceed, Mr. Kobs."

"Professor Sheridan?"

"There was a gradual movement out of the Dark Ages and into feudal times where power, even in the presence of a king, was mostly in the hands of local squires. Over time, power was consolidated and wielded by a single absolute ruler, so that by the seventeenth and eighteenth centuries this form of governance was prevalent."

"Would you explain the meaning of absolute in this context?"

"Certainly. The king held absolute power over all land and over all life. Turned around, it means that everyone's land and their very life were kept at the king's whim."

"How did an absolute ruler manage his kingdom?"

"In a word, through the court. By court I don't mean the place or a building, but the people, the lesser nobility and the courtiers who were required to attend on the king, or who wanted something."

"How did the court operate?"

"The king dispensed everything he chose to dispense within the court: land, titles and honors, benefits, appointments. The list goes on and on. By keeping all that in the court, the king built on the royal mystique, secured his power, and stifled potential opposition. I might add that rewards were based on loyalty, not necessarily on merit or competence."

"How was this mystique of absolute power promoted?"

"In many, many ways." The witness paused in thought. "First there were all the trappings calculated to impress: the titles, for example Your Most Serene Highness; thrones and throne rooms; crowns and coronations; romantic promotion of royal weddings and births; winter and summer palaces; ornate and expensive clothing; jeweled and gold jewelry. All went to enhance the mystique of specialness.

"Next there were the court protocols. For example, lesser royals and courtiers actually vied with one another to assist the monarch when he got out of bed in the morning, when he went to bed at night, and even when he relieved himself. Court ritual and etiquette addressed every moment of a royal's existence.

"Finally, the mystique was promoted by the church. Theologians developed the theory of the divine right of kings, which legitimized a king's right over life and land. The king was God's vicar in the temporal order just as the pope was in the spiritual order. The pope also was an absolute ruler in his own temporal kingdom."

"How did the papal kingdom match up against, oh, say, Louis XIV's kingdom?"

"In format they were identical. The pope was an absolute ruler in the papal states. He ruled through his court, dispensing land, benefits, and, obviously, spiritual gifts. Again, land and life were at his whim. Like other rulers, the accepted morality of the time permitted the pope to torture and kill. We see that exemplified in the Crusades and the Inquisition. Also, the higher positions of the clergy, cardinals and bishops, were customarily filled from the nobility. And, raised in the aristocratic culture, they supported it fully without question or consciousness of alternatives."

"What specifically distinguished the nobility from the rest of humankind?"

"At first it was simply power. Then, over the centuries, the distinguishing mark became a matter of bloodline. They claimed to be an exclusive caste by virtue of blood. Genealogies were treasured — and sometimes contrived. Napoleon was the first commoner to breach this system at the most exalted level."

"Were the nobility really noble?"

"Only if you accept the blood distinction. For the most part, the aristocracy was a fairly shallow lot. They concerned themselves with gossip, parlor games, entertainments, sport, intrigue, and of course, their genealogies. They were self-absorbed to the point of ignoring anything outside their particular culture. Within that culture all the tools of intrigue were practiced regardless of their morality."

"If you were to capture the essence of that royal culture in a few words, what would they be?"

"It was a culture based on pretense, the mystique of a ruler who, by the grace of God, or so they claimed, controlled everything at his pleasure. As a consequence, sycophancy defined the society because any ambition could only be advanced in that manner. The culture was exploitative, belittling, and pompous. Trivia, as in the rules of etiquette, replaced anything of substance."

"One final question. What was the relationship of the nobility to the masses?"

"The masses were totally discounted. They were peasants whose role was that of tax provider and cannon fodder. The reality is that the rest of humankind did not enter the nobility's consciousness. If they ever noticed the dire poverty and terrible suffering of the masses they did little more than raise a perfumed handkerchief to their nose and thank God they were not of that estate. As they were nobility by the grace of God, so the grace of God had ordained that the others were established in their misery."

"Thank you, Dr. Sheridan. No further questions. Your witness, Mr. Goulding."

Goulding sat at the prosecution table shaking his head. He stood, but stayed at the table. "Dr. Sheridan, would you say that those royals were insane?"

"I have no competence in that area. I can say that, immersed as I am in my own culture, I would hate to live in that culture, or to be a member of that society."

"No further questions at this time, Your Honor," Goulding said. "I wish to reserve the right to recall this witness should Mr. Kobs attempt to make her testimony relevant."

JACOB

The trial goes faster if I let my mind drift now and then. I don't often go into my imagination, but lately Inez has given me cause to do that. She is a princess with a fox to tame. Like the little prince, she waits at a distance, but not silently. Words are always in the air, words calculated to win trust, sharing words. So it is words and wait. And I can't keep myself from imagining outcomes.

I don't doubt that Inez will win Deenah's trust. I was a much more difficult challenge in that regard even though the abuse dealt me was far less damaging than Deenah's. She was twice wounded, once where trust made her a willing partner only to be betrayed. She is a survivor.

The healing is happening before my eyes. Watching Inez with Deenah is like watching a physician peel away a dreadful scar and reveal the fresh and tender underlayment. Inez tries to credit me, but my part is inconsequential. I'm backdrop, a man with no facility with words, no ability to read a need in either myself or others and select the healing phrase. I try only to make Deenah feel welcome with us. Then I follow Inez's lead.

Deenah is shy and withdrawn, a bird confined to the ground, looking for the confidence to fly. Fly she will if Inez has her way. I want them both to succeed. Face it, Jacob. You were wounded and you flew. You know something of what Deenah is going through. She is a pretty girl, and as I get to know her, the prettiness goes deeper and deeper. She's bright. Inez says she was nearly a straight A student in high school.

Inez is always up. Even so, there's added animation in her since Deenah. The need to heal is in her. As I listen to this trial, I can't sense any of that need in these bishops. If Deenah is to come out whole, it won't come from them or their peers. Probably just the opposite. For her to approach them would most likely get her revictimized. According to the testimony I've heard here, I'm not the only one to have experienced that. When I think of my mother and dad, I — don't think about it, Jacob.

I don't pray much in the way of asking. God's been good to Inez and me. But I have started praying for Deenah, that she permits us to help her, and that what we do does help. That's what Inez wants. And that's what I want for both their sakes.

Chapter Fourteen

Monsignor Dino Piacenza's bald head, round face, energetic eyes, and smile faced Kobs from the witness stand.

"Please state your qualifications, Monsignor," Kobs said.

"I have a doctorate in Roman Catholic Theology from the Gregorian University in Rome. I have for the past twenty-two years specialized in the history of heraldic symbols and ceremony, and am considered an expert in protocol."

"By protocol you mean?"

"Protocol is defined as 'the customs and regulations dealing with diplomatic formality, precedence and etiquette.' As to my expertise, I might add that I have been a consultant on protocol to the Vatican and to the diplomatic corps of twenty-two nations. I have published three works on heraldic symbols and protocol."

"Your enthusiasm for the subject is evident, Monsignor. You mentioned formality, precedence, etiquette, heraldry, and ceremony. Aren't those usually associated with court life?"

"Yes, they are."

"Is there a papal court?"

"No and yes. Let me explain, please. Historians have determined a papal court existed at least from the seventh century. It has possessed its full grandeur since the early fourteenth century, the Renaissance. In a moment of perhaps democratic sentiment, Pope Paul VI in his 1968 *motu proprio, Pontificalis Domus,* reorganized the Roman Curia and renamed some of the functions. What was the papal court is now subsumed under the titles *Papal Household* and *Papal Chapel.*

"I see. Just how substantial were these changes?"

"Oh, the church eliminated some Vatican posts and titles that had lost relevance. In some cases the posts were irrelevant and eliminated, but titles were retained."

"How were the laity and hierarchy affected by the changes?"

"With regard to the laity, prior to Pope Paul's action, pontiffs regularly granted noble titles such as prince, duke, marquis, and count to deserving lay people. Most people, for example, are unaware that an American woman received the title, duchess, from Pope Pius XII through the mediation of Cardinal Spellman. Since Pope Paul's *motu proprio*, former titles are no longer bestowed, though some individuals retain those previously awarded. Other titles such as Stewards of St. Peter and Gentleman of His Holiness are now in use. Of course, the many classes of knights have been retained."

"Like the Knights of Columbus?"

"In a sense like them, though the Knights of Columbus were founded in New Haven, Connecticut in 1882, and membership does not flow from a papal award. The Knights of Columbus in this country might be used as an honor guard in processions, going ahead of the altar boys, but precedence would go to seminarians, priests, prelates, and any of the papal orders of knights."

"You are not putting down the Knights of Columbus?"

"Oh, my, no. They do much good. But they are not among the papal knights."

"Are there many papal orders of knights?"

"Yes, many."

"Back to the changes of Pope Paul VI. How were the hierarchy affected?"

"Very little."

"Would you give an example?"

"Let me think a moment — Yes. Take the cardinals, for example. Cardinals have been around for centuries, and their roles today are much as they were in the ninth century. The Congress of Vienna, which concluded the Napoleonic Wars in 1814–1815, confirmed that cardinals are equal in rank to princes of the royal blood, having precedence immediately after crown princes. This diplomatic recognition was ratified as recently as the Versailles Treaty, which ended World War I. A cardinal is therefore accorded the title of 'Your Eminence.' "

Kobs walked to a slide projector and flipped the switch. A display of various coats of arms shown on the screen. "I'm sure you will recognize these hierarchical coats of arms, Monsignor. Would you explain for us how these heraldic symbols carry the notions of rank and precedence?"

Piacenza looked over the examples, his smile enlarging as his eyes moved from one to the other. "Easily," he said. "The *fiocchi*!"

"Fee-yo-kee?"

"Yes. They are the little tassels strung together on each side of the insignia. You see them in the shape of something like a Christmas tree. On the upper left coat of arms you see fifteen *fiocchi* on each side. They are colored scarlet. One knows immediately that this coat belongs to a cardinal. The one to the right with ten green *fiocchi* is that of an archbishop. And the one below with six green *fiocchi* belongs to a bishop."

Kobs looked directly at Monsignor Piacenza, his face innocent of expression. "Thank God for *fiocchi*, eh, Monsignor?"

"Indeed, yes. So colorful and enchanting."

"Would it be correct then to say that the style of the hierarchy is similar to that of the old royal courts of Europe?"

"Oh, yes indeed. In fact it is often difficult to know who borrowed what from whom in terms of heraldry, etiquette, and ceremony."

"Do you find other royal influences in the hierarchy?"

"But of course. In liturgical ceremonies one sees the throne, the royal garb, the exquisite etiquette of bows, genuflection, and kneeling. The life of the Church is filled with reflections of the nobility and its etiquette."

"By church, do you mean the people or the hierarchy?"

"Well, the people certainly have their place, but this protocol, this heraldry and enchanting etiquette belongs to the realm of the hierarchy."

"Realm?"

"Yes, as in kingdom."

"In summation thus far, Monsignor, can we say that the Church's royal, hierarchical culture is alive and well today?"

"But of course."

"A purple culture?"

"What a wonderful metaphor, so colorful, so, so apt."

"Tell us more about hierarchical etiquette, please, Monsignor."

"Well, let's look at the funeral and burial etiquette surrounding the death of a cardinal —"

LILITH

I can't help but reminisce. I've been Robert's housekeeper, and cook, and laundress, and companion for nearly twenty years, ever since he became a pastor and then when he was rector of the seminary. Such a lovely house we had on the seminary grounds!

Living with him was almost like living with silence. Our conversations were mostly about household matters and books. Thank God for my degree in literature. I was able to recommend novels to Robert and we would discuss them at table sometimes. He was always into books. I thought his sermons were too abstract and intellectual, and once I told him that. When we were living at the seminary, I decided to further my education and get a degree in theology. I thought that might let me enter his life a little more. So I commuted to Loyola University on a part-time basis and over six years obtained my master's degree. That helped our relationship, and I think it was good for both of us. We could converse on Robert's level on the subject closest to his heart.

Robert never had many friends. He was something of a loner with little social life outside of the two of us and a few members of the clergy. I have always had several close women friends and we frequently lunch, converse, and go to the theater. Robert never went to the theater.

I am so upset by this trial. I'm convinced that the prosecutor totally convinced the jury of their guilt. He convinced me that all three of them were neglectful at best, but that's me, trying to put the best possible light on it for Robert's sake. The sexual abuse described by the prosecutor was horrible, but I'm sure Robert never connected to the horror of it.

I can't make sense of all this. Attorney Kobs is trying to convince the jury that all three are insane. Robert isn't insane. I've never known a more rational person. He's always in his head. He's a man of routine and syllogisms. How can that be insane? I've lived with my brother for the past nineteen years and I've never seen him in a moment of unintended behavior. He's not crazy by any standard of sanity I've known. Maybe I don't understand insanity, like I don't understand sex.

He's not evil either. He knows the commandments and he knows the Church's canons. If he's ever violated any of them, I've never witnessed the transgression. Robert is a good man as I understand goodness. He dedicated himself to the Church with the clear conviction that to serve the Church is to serve God. How can that connect him to evil? I think I know his heart. There's no evil there that I can see. Maybe I don't understand evil. If it's not in the heart, where is it?

BEN BAUER

Ben followed his parish group of fourteen adults into Holy Name Cathedral. The event was the annual gathering of all adult candidates for baptism in the archdiocese currently engaged in their preparation studies. Today Cardinal Timothy Thompson will greet them, welcome them to the Catholic community, and encourage them in the study of the faith. Scheduled for baptism at the next year's Easter vigil, and still unfamiliar with the Catholic environment, they entered the pews timidly, some taking furtive glances around the spacious church. Soon some twelve hundred candidates would nearly fill the church's capacity of fifteen hundred.

Curly Ward, Ben's classmate and the wit of their class, motioned people into the space behind Ben's group and slipped into the pew next to Ben, to the side of their groups. The two shook hands.

"Ready for the Eminence?" Curly whispered.

"Had the full dose a month or so ago, Curly." Ben replied.

The organist began playing "Amazing Grace," signaling the audience to rise and the beginning of the procession. An altar boy carrying the archiepiscopal cross, and two candle bearers led the procession. A sizeable group of pastors, vested in cassock and surplice, followed. Behind them, the cardinal, thudding his crozier into the stone floor, beamed a smile from side to side.

"You should be out there, Ben," Curly murmured.

"I'm happy right here," Ben replied.

"Bet you a ten spot Timothy talks about Timothy."

"It's a sin to bet on a sure thing, Curly."

The cardinal arrived at the ambo and looked out at the crowd with a broad smile. "Since you are just learning about our faith, ladies and gentlemen, you may be wondering who that character with the funny hat up here is."

The crowd tittered.

"Well, he's a human being like yourselves, got arms and legs like everybody else. But we are the successors of the apostles, nonetheless."

Right, Ben thought. Bishops didn't show up until the end of the first century. A small jump there to be successors. All of these people are successors of the apostles.

"You may not know that bishops have been considered royalty since the time of Constantine. In the year three hundred twelve the emperor declared the bishop of Rome to be such and gave him his very own palace in Rome, known as the Lateran Palace. Over the centuries all bishops became regarded as royalty. You may know that in some Christian denominations bishops are still addressed as Your Lordship. In the Roman Catholic church, cardinals are addressed as Your Eminence and bishops as Your Excellency.

"You're not writing this down, Ben?" Curly asked.

Ben shrugged his shoulders.

"A bishop's church is called a cathedral. If you will all look up at the ceiling you will see the coat of arms of Cardinal John Cody, the eminence who restored this cathedral nearly fifty years ago. You can tell that is a cardinal's coat of arms because there are fifteen scarlet tassels on each side. My coat of arms has fifteen scarlet tassels —"

The true cathedral, Ben thought, is the compassionate man or woman.

Curly groaned audibly.

Ben jabbed an elbow into Curly's ribs.

Cardinal Thompson removed the mitre from his head and held it up for inspection. He embarked on a lengthy explanation of its connection to early Greek athletes and drew a hesitant titter from the audience when he flexed his right arm. He followed that with an equally long discourse on the relation of his crozier and rings to his authority. "For centuries, etiquette required that people of lesser rank kneel and kiss the bishop's ring as a sign of their submission."

"Whoop de dooey," from Curly. "God help me. And what would Jesus say to that?"

Ben glanced at his candidates and saw puzzlement in their wrinkled brows and eyes.

Curly grabbed Ben's sleeve. "If I knew what a petard was I would hoist myself on it. Kill me, Ben, please."

Ben was unable to totally smother his laughter.

Thompson went on. "I've had a large replica of my coat of arms placed in the narthex for your observation. A few words now to help you understand the various insignia —"

When the cardinal left the ambo and proceeded to the narthex, Curly turned to Ben. "Okay, Ben. You're the smartest guy in our class. Give me a one-sentence summary. Or is it impossible to summarize trivia?"

Ben shook his head, laughing. "Take care of yourself, Curly. I owe you one. Your running commentary helped me get through that." As he walked from the church the summary came: It's all about me!

Chapter Fifteen

Kobs stood next to the witness stand, attentive to the occupant's statement.

"Thank you, Dr. Hinger. After that recitation, I'm confident the jury recognizes your expertise on the subject of addiction."

The witness nodded, a smile on his benign face.

"How is addiction defined?" Kobs began.

"Addictions can be either substance or process addictions. The addiction is the state one is in when the particular substance or process has taken control over their life, and over which the person is powerless."

"By substance you mean something like drugs or alcohol?"

"That is correct."

"Give us examples of processes that can be addictive."

"Certainly. Processes like gambling, making money, sex, and work are examples."

"How does a person become an addict? I mean, what leads him or her into that state?"

"The substance or process acts as a lure, an implicit promise that it will solve or protect from whatever interior problems the person feels helpless against."

"How does a clinical practitioner, such as yourself, detect with certainty that a client is addicted?"

"There is a syndrome, that is, a complex of symptoms attached to the disease."

"What sort of symptoms?"

"Defense mechanisms like denial where the addict always denies he is addicted, or projection where the problem is always someone else's problem. Also, there are symptoms like self-centeredness, a need to control the environs so that the fix is always available; ethical regression or degeneration where the addict will lie, cheat, or steal for the fix; distorted thinking; blocked emotions — the list goes on."

"Thank you. We may come back to some of those. But first, can a culture be addictive?

"I would have to reflect on that. An organization can be addictive. A good example of that is in the relation between a person addicted to work and the organization he works for. They feed on each other."

JUROR #1

God almighty, he's talking about Andy. It brings back the scene when my sister, Rosie, announced that she was engaged to marry the guy. The whole family liked Andy. He was a bit stiff, but a hell of a hard worker, a good lawyer. Rosie was in seventh heaven. And we knew she'd make a great mom and he'd be a sure provider. They'd make a great pair.

And that's the way it was for the first couple years. I was close to Rosie. We'd meet downtown for coffee once a week. As the kids came along, she'd bring them with her.

After a few years, I began to see trouble in Rosie's eyes. Nothing was ever wrong, of course. She was just worried about Andy. He was working too hard, spending too much time at the office. "He's only thinking of you and the kids, Rosie," I remember saying. The comment won me a clouded look.

The company held out rewards, lures like this expert is talking about. Andy got sucked in. He began a move up the fast track. As time went on, Rosie's complaints mounted. Andy was never home. Never had time for the kids. He'd miss events important to them. If she complained to him, his standard reply was he was doing it all for her and the kids. She'd grown used to an affluent lifestyle, he told her. He was only trying to insure that for her, and debt-free college for the kids.

One day Rosie hit him with the fact she didn't want the lifestyle just for herself, or debt-free college for the kids if it meant they didn't have time for each other. He couldn't stop now, he told her. He was almost there. There, being the head of the legal department. She didn't care about that, she told him. She wanted him around. He turned the blame on her, just like this witness is saying. She was the selfish one. She couldn't hold up her end. Her end being the home and the kids. Rosie swallowed that crap and backed off.

Three years later the corporation promoted Andy to head the legal department. He had made it. But now there were only two corporate layers above him. He set a new goal, the next layer, just another version of his fix. The corporation had total control of him.

One by one the kids went off to college having known their dad only from a distance, distance even on the rare times they were together. Rosie drifted into volunteer work and became a docent at the art museum. Andy seldom came home anymore. He had an apartment near the office. Rosie learned that his excuses had become easy lies.

Andy was up for an executive vice president position when the crash came. The corporation was heavy into acquisitions, and a young lawyer, trusted by Andy, made some kind of math error. The mistake put the company in a vulnerable position and would be damaging cost-wise. The document had crossed Andy's desk, but he had only scanned it under other pressures. The remedy was costly. Andy fired the guilty subordinate and maneuvered to shift blame away from himself.

It didn't work. Like this guy is saying, the corporate culture expected perfection and even assumed it was possible. A couple weeks went by and Andy started to feel like he had survived. The corporate heads had only used the time to select a replacement. Andy's termination was quick and final.

I can only imagine Andy's feelings then. He had given his life to this corporation and they couldn't tolerate a single mistake. He got in his Mercedes and drove north to Wisconsin. Two days later police found the car in a parking area next to Lake Michigan. A week later, a sport fisherman, trolling for salmon, came upon Andy's floating, bloated body. Police concluded that Andy had parked, got out of the car without turning off the engine, and walked straight into the lake. He couldn't swim!

It must have been like this guy is saying. When the job ended, there was no more Andy. He had thought to fill himself up from the outside, from corporate success and recognition. When that outside no longer recognized him, he didn't exist even to himself. God, how awful.

When I look at these bishops, I don't see them as hard workers. I wonder where Kobs is going with this?

"Professor Hinger," Kobs asked, "if an organization can be addictive, wouldn't the culture of that organization be part of the addictive substance and process?"

"Ah, I see your point. You are restricting the word culture from the general sense, as in western culture, to a definite and restricted group of people, as in, for example, a corporate culture. And of course, the answer is yes."

"How would you know whether someone is addicted to a particular organization and its culture?"

"The syndrome is essentially the same as for any addiction with, perhaps, a few additions."

"Such as?"

"The message goes out that the institution comes first. Its survival is paramount. It is expected that conventional morality can be compromised in that pursuit. This priority given the organization's culture leads to an attempt to control everything and everyone in the organization. One does not question the culture and the policies that support it. A sense of interior perfection also prevents the insiders from accepting intelligence from the outside."

"But many of these organizations are often civic minded, are they not?"

"Yes, of course. They want to project the perfect image. They will donate money and assign staff to assist civic and charitable works. They spin the organization as caring, as a good neighbor who understands the human condition and prevailing circumstances. The organization will form committees from the outside for input, but the committee recommendations go nowhere. They conclude with feasts and festivities, thanks and congratulations, but nothing more."

"Okay on that." Kobs paused. "Isn't an institution or organization actually the people who run it, the top tiers? Doesn't saying the institution comes first mean that the top tier comes first and their survival is paramount?"

"It is possible, yes."

"Let's turn our attention back to the addict. What is the mental state of a true addict?"

"I see it as a species of insanity. Let me explain. If you see all of the symptoms together in action, the addict is more than dysfunctional. Morally, he is functionally insane. When the break with conventional morality occurs, when that morality is replaced by a personal exemption, the addict is disconnected from reality and is insane."

"Thank you, Professor Hinger. No further questions, Your Honor."

"Your witness, Mr. Goulding."

"Professor Hinger," Goulding began, "the illusion that Mr. Kobs is trying to create here, that bishops are insane because they are bishops, do you agree with that?"

"I've never thought about it."

"Do you think Roman Catholics are insane?"

"No, certainly not the ones I know well."

"So, membership in a religious organization doesn't carry with it the connotation of insanity?"

"Not in the sense of the entire Catholic population."

"Can religion be addictive?"

"Yes, both as a substance and as a process. But that doesn't mean that every religious person is an addict or is insane."

Frustration flickered on Goulding's face. "All right, give some examples where religion might be addictive as a substance or as a process."

"Where you find moral deterioration, for example. Fanatical groups within a major religion who will kill because their interpretation of its message permits or encourages it. We see examples of that daily in the press. A cult might be another example. There the group's commitment to the leader may call for immoral acts. Immoral by conventional standards but not in their eyes."

"All right. The hierarchy of bishops in the Roman Catholic Church is a relatively small group, several thousand worldwide. In your professional opinion, do they constitute a group of addicts?"

"I have never examined the behavior of the hierarchy. I'm not competent to answer that question."

"An opinion is all I'm asking for, Professor. If anyone exists who has the competence to give an opinion here, it is you. You must have an opinion."

"No. I do not."

BEN BAUER

Ben picked up the phone. "Hey, Johnny, how goes the renowned pastor of Holy Polish Martyrs?"

"Not good, Ben. Listen, can you meet Curly and me for lunch tomorrow? I gotta talk to you guys."

Ben heard the troubled urgency in John's tone of voice. "Just tell me where and when. I'll be there, Johnny."

An older crowd frequented Hallie's Family Restaurant and the Bing Crosby-era music was muted. Conversation was possible. Ben, Curly, and John Kozlowski occupied a booth.

"Timothy Thompson wants title of the parish turned over to his corporation sole," John began. "As you know, corporation sole is legalese for whoever the archbishop is who happens to head the archdiocese. He's laying the pressure on the trustees. And, naturally, he's telling them that he will only hold the property 'in trust' for the people of the parish. He's starting the pressure by trying to woo them. You know, explaining the benefits of such a transfer."

"Like what benefits?" Curly asked.

"Like the archdiocese having the property to increase its asset base and thereby its borrowing power. The borrowing would, of course, be used for the benefit of the people — as in helping poorer parishes build their facilities."

"Or for expensive remodeling of the episcopal residence," Curly added. "But certainly not for compensating victims of clergy sexual abuse."

"Those items are never mentioned," John replied. "Anyway, the trustees aren't buying into his spin."

"What he really wants is control," Ben said. "If he has control, the people can't walk away from the archdiocese and take their property with them."

"He just wants to hold it in trust, does he?" Curly added. "Why doesn't he trust the people for once? Never mind. I know the answer."

"Corporation sole has title over every other parish in the archdiocese," Ben said. "You mean that Holy Martyrs parish somehow escaped the episcopal plundering?"

"As near as I can figure, it happened when the throne was empty — more than a hundred years ago," John said. "The archbishop had died. Holy Polish Martyrs was dedicated by an auxiliary bishop in the interim. The title was put in the name of the parish trustees from the moment they started construction."

"That's something!" Curly said, serious for a moment.

"How did they get by with that for all these decades? Didn't other archbishops go after them?"

"Just about every one of them. The trustees kept saying no. I suppose the archbishops thought it wasn't worth the fight. We Poles can be stubborn, you know."

"In your case, that's an understatement," Curly joshed.

"I don't understand it. If you go way back, a few years before Holy Martyrs parish ever existed, the people out at St. Stan's built their church. It was up and ready for two years, unused, because the archbishop wouldn't consecrate it until he got title," John said. "Anyway, however this situation came about, that's the way it is."

"And the problem is, Thompson's on your back."

"Yeah, big time. But I really don't give a damn about Thompson. I'm worried about the parish. I'm concerned this issue might split the people. Right now we're a pretty tight group. I don't need a cardinal screwing that up because he uses canon law to satisfy his own ego."

"You're strong on this, right?" Curly asked.

"You bet I am," John replied. "It's extortion. It's theft, pure and simple, but Thompson doesn't see it that way. He thinks that God backs every move the hierarchy makes. They can put a law on the books that extends their authority to all Church property and thereby legitimize their authority to take it. Put the trustees under interdict, no problem. Put the entire parish under interdict, no problem. Take away their priest, no problem. Deprive the people of the sacraments, no problem. I don't care how you translate it, that's extortion. Extortion by threat."

"What's Thompson threatening you with, Johnny?" Ben asked.

"Removal as pastor."

"What would your people say about that?"

"You can never tell, but we have a strong bond. There's a lot of goodwill out there for me. I feel it all the time. My best guess is they will go where I will lead them."

"What are you going to do?" Curly asked.

"I'm going to tell the trustees about the threat. Then I'm going to tell them I'm on their side whatever their decision. If they want to tell Timothy Thompson to go to hell, I won't try to dissuade them. If Timothy Thompson tries to remove me, I'll put it to the people. If they want me to stay, I'll stay. I've had enough of this imperial crap."

"And then Thompson will put you and the entire parish under interdict. No sacraments and all the rest of it," Ben said.

"I know that, Ben. But I'll keep doing what I've been doing, sacraments and all. It's not the way I want it, but I'll do it. Somebody's got to stand up for what we are supposed to be all about."

"I'm on Thompson's shit list already, Johnny," Ben said. "I don't think he'd accept me as a mediator of any kind. Is that what you want Curly and me to be?"

"No. I just want my two closest friends to tell me if I'm off base."

Ben put a hand on his shoulder. "I'm not sure I'd have the balls to do it, Johnny, but I hope I would. I admire your courage and I'm with you all the way."

"Ditto," Curly said.

Chapter Sixteen

Kobs called his next witness to the stand. John Melloh testified that he held master's degrees in social work and in psychology, and had worked for the past twenty-six years in the study of cults and in the rescue of cult members. A hulk of a man, his dark eyes peered out from the shade of bushy, black eyebrows. His bearing reflected an inner calm.

"Mr. Melloh, what exactly is a cult?" Kobs asked.

"There are many definitions out there," Melloh responded. "But essentially cult members will exhibit complete and unquestioning allegiance to their leader, who will in turn manipulate and exploit those same members, often inflicting harm on them and on society."

"Who would join a cult?"

"Anyone can be lured in. Old and young, rich and poor, intelligent or not."

"How does it happen that someone joins a cult?"

"The cult promises to respond to some need such as dependency, idealism, a way out of disillusion, a search for meaning or spirituality, things like that."

"How does the cult entrap new members?" Kobs asked. "I presume we are talking here of entrapment."

"Yes, we are," Melloh replied. "The cult leader makes promises as I mentioned. The group presents itself as special, elitist. It is always centered around a living leader who requires absolute submission. Questioning and dissent are forbidden. A recruit is indoctrinated on how to feel and think. Behavior is controlled, sometimes to the minutest detail. In short, the cult entraps new members by any and all methods of mind control."

"Once in, how do they get out?"

"They don't often get out. But sometimes disillusionment caused by abuse may lead them out. Mostly those who get out are helped by some sort of outside intervention."

"So getting out is not easy?"

"Far from it. The recruit enters a box, and from the inside they see no exit. A cult demands total commitment and employs a variety of techniques to keep the box sealed."

"Such as?"

"Such as constant required indoctrination, constant activities of some sort, guilt, things like that. Remember, once a person commits to membership they already feel, think, and behave as the cult leader prescribes."

"Can a church be a cult?"

"Yes. Many cults use the word church in their self-identification —"

INEZ

Inez sat listening to the testimony. She held Deenah's hand. Thirty-year-old memories crowded her imagination. Pictures of her friend Maria's oldest daughter, Debbie, along with Debbie's story marched through her memory.

Inez and Maria were as close as twins, defenders of the other against any foe. Maria, dark haired and given to weight. Inez, thin and fair with golden hair. Debbie resembled Inez in figure and in fairness. And Debbie was the light in both friends' eyes. Inez doted on her and left discipline to Maria and Maria's husband, Aldo.

Growing up, Debbie's disposition was consistently sunny. She was warm and affectionate, and had a host of friends. A high-school cheerleader, she was also life's cheerleader. Inez recalled some of their laughter-filled, lighthearted conversations with an aching heart.

Exceptionally bright, Debbie won a full scholarship at the state university, although her affluent parents could easily have afforded tuition. She excelled through all of her freshman year. Inez first sensed a dampening in Debbie's spirit during a family Christmas celebration in her sophomore year, but ascribed it to any one of the temporary disappointments we all endure over time.

At spring break that same school year, at a luncheon with Debbie, Inez intuited a deepening of the girl's withdrawal. In conversation with Maria later, she learned of the mother's growing alarm. Debbie had joined some group and was deeply involved in their mission. The girl's conversation was flooded with words of praise and wonder at the wisdom of the group's leader. By this time, Debbie had finished a six-month initiation period and was already a full-fledged member. Her grades had dropped precipitously and she was now barely passing. She left home after only three days to return to the group.

When the school year ended, Debbie came home and announced that the group leader would be coming to visit. He was now her boyfriend. "You will be amazed at his wisdom," she told her mother. "He has the most awesome spirituality."

Inez and Jacob were visiting Maria and Aldo when the young man of twenty-eight arrived. He was dressed in levis and a tee shirt emblazoned front and back with ULTIMATE CONSCIOUSNESS! He called Debbie, Maia.

"I have a new name," Debbie announced. "Isn't Maia beautiful?"

Beautiful maybe, Inez had thought. But certainly not original. She wondered if this modern oldest daughter of Atlas and the mother by Zeus of Hermes, the god of cunning and theft, held any symbolic significance. Did the young man consider himself the modern Zeus?

"Master gives each new member a new name," Debbie explained.

"*Master?*" Maria asked.

"Yes. That is his only name now," Debbie said.

"Tell us about your group," Inez asked, turning to Master.

"We are seeker of this," he said in a resonant voice, pointing at his shirt.

"And what exactly is ultimate consciousness?" Debbie's father asked, trying to hide his dismay and skepticism.

"Ultimate consciousness is love, truth, and beauty at their fullness," he replied.

"And how does one achieve this ultimate consciousness?" Jacob asked.

"By following me," Master said, a hint of challenge in his voice.

"What does following you entail?" Jacob again.

"Total obedience," he replied.

"Without questions?" Jacob again.

"Yes. Doubt and questioning are among the greatest obstacles to ultimate consciousness."

"What sort of credentials do you have?" Jacob asked.

"Those who listen to my words with the fullness of faith will know in their hearts that I already possess ultimate consciousness. That is my only credential."

"Why would you not respond to rational questions about your claim of ultimate consciousness?" Aldo asked. "It seems that you have insulated yourself from the demands of reason. Or have I missed something here?"

Master gave his audience a brief glimpse of disdain. "My words speak to the listener's heart and are heard only there. If anyone listens with their mind expecting rational discourse, they will not receive the gift I speak of. Rational thought is like doubt and questioning, an insurmountable obstacle on the road to ultimate consciousness."

"Interesting," Inez commented, and turned the conversation to summer matters.

After several days, Master returned to his group. Debbie followed, but not before deriding her parents and Inez for not recognizing the truth about Master, something she considered the absolute height of disrespect. She had fully expected them to stand in awe and to fall in line.

Maria said, "Debbie, we love you. We want you to be happy."

"You will call me Maia. That is my name now," the girl demanded.

"Your friends are all asking about you," Maria said.

"I have new friends now. I've grown up. Please understand that."

Maria, Inez, Aldo, and Jacob began a search for a way to rescue Debbie. Upon recommendations and close examination, they were drawn to a professional group who were in the business of rescuing cult members. The professionals held responsible degrees or were former cult members themselves. They could and would deprogram Debbie from the forces that held her to the cult. Their method would involve the forced confinement of Debbie in a secure location and a process of instruction on the brainwashing and mind control methods of the cult. The program had a reasonable success rate. Today, Inez reflected, the methods are less coercive.

The intervention never happened. The cult wrapped itself around their Maia and kept even her parents at bay. Within a year the cult vanished from the state. Rumors floated that it was either in Northern California, Montana, or Oregon. Several years later, Maria and Aldo received an envelope postmarked from Denver. It contained only a picture: A shabbily dressed and obviously pregnant Debbie with a baby at her breast. Years later, a detective hired by the family found the group. By then Master had a new mate. Debbie had vanished. Cult members said she had simply left with a man assigned as her new mate by Master. There was no trail.

Inez felt the tears on her cheeks. I'm not Catholic, she thought, but could the pope be like Master and the bishops like Debbie?

LILITH

Armed with the freedom and insights given me by my exposure to
the worlds of literature and theology, I came to enjoy challenging
Robert. I'm not sure he enjoyed the experience. Earlier, my percep-
tions of reality had been restricted by all the forces of my training:
family, Church, ethnic neighborhood, and educator-censored reading. My enlarged horizons compelled me to question everything,
even Robert's Catholic assumptions.

One evening at dinner we had a conversation that puts flesh on
the testimony of Mr. Melloh. I remember going over that conversation in my mind again and again. Robert managed to close every
point of dispute. Box is a wonderful metaphor for what I heard.

"I understand from my reading, Robert, that bishops are expected
to boldly question and challenge the beliefs and behavior of even
presidents and kings," I said. "Is that correct?"

"Yes it is, Lilith," he said.

"Shouldn't you also question and challenge the beliefs and moral
judgments of your superiors, the pope and the Curia, if you disagree
with them?"

"One does not question either the Holy Father or the Holy See,
Lilith."

"Why not?"

"You wouldn't understand."

"Why wouldn't I understand?

"You're a woman."

"What's that got to do with anything? I'm at least as smart as you.
In fact, my grades were always better — if that matters." I had almost lost myself to anger.

"I meant you are not a member of the clergy. On becoming a
bishop, I was obligated to take the 'Oath of Fidelity.' In that oath I
swore absolute loyalty to the Holy Father. That includes loyalty to his

appointed members of the Holy See, the Curia. And obviously it also includes absolute obedience to approved Church teaching and to Church law."

"What if some of that teaching is wrong, or some of those laws are unjust?"

"Error is not possible. God sees to that."

"What about centuries of the Inquisition, the papal-sponsored burning of witches, the horrors of the papal-endorsed Crusades with its promise of salvation for the killing of infidels, the slaughter of so-called heretics like the Albigenses, and Church tolerance if not sponsorship of pogroms against the Jews?"

"We can't relive the past, Lilith, or judge it."

"We should," I said. "How else will we learn from it?"

Robert tilted his head back and eyed me, a severe expression on his face. "I'm beginning to worry about you, Lilith. Jesus promised that he would send the Holy Spirit to guide his Church. He did send the Spirit who is with us now. He is the guarantor that the Church will not fall into error."

I wasn't to be put off. "Maybe by Church, Jesus meant the people. Maybe the Holy Spirit is talking to you bishops and to the pope through the wisdom of the laity."

"Really!" Robert actually look affronted. "And what would the Holy Spirit be telling Christ's authorized spiritual leaders through the laity?"

"Maybe He's saying you're wrong about such matters as birth control, married and women priests, a monarchical-style hierarchy, things like that."

"Lilith, I consider myself a servant of the laity. But, it is I who have the teaching authority — competence if you will — not the laity."

I gave him back his. "Really! You have nothing to learn?"

"Of course I must learn."

"But not from the laity?"

"My source is the Holy Father. I have no other authority over me."

"You and the pope and the so-called Holy See are simply afraid to say you have made mistakes in faith and morals. You see your entire hierarchical structure falling into ruin if you do so. I don't see competency in that attitude."

"Lilith, I am tied to the Holy Father with a rope of steel. And that's the way I see things, and that's the way I choose to be."

"Is that like a leash?"

"If you wish."

"You see the laity's role in the old cliché 'pay, pray, and obey'?"

"Essentially, yes. Of course there are some administrative areas where their abilities are useful."

"Really!"

Bill Goulding stood to the side of the witness stand, his eyes down, his face thoughtful and toward the jury. He raised his eyes and turned to the witness. "Mr. Melloh," he began. "The defense attorney seems to want us all to believe that the Roman Catholic church is a cult. Would you agree that it is a cult?"

"No. I'm quite certain that it is not a cult."

"Oh? On what do you base that conclusion."

"On my personal experience. I am a Roman Catholic, and I know from my associations in the Church that many members are not laboring under any sort of mind control."

"How do you know that?"

"Members that I know personally are independent thinkers with independent consciences. And not just a few. Eighty percent of us disagree with Church teaching on birth control. Nearly that many disagree on matters such as women and married priests, property confiscation, things like that."

"Is it possible that smaller groups within — No. Forget that." Goulding caught himself, envisioning a counterproductive path of questions. "No further questions," he said.

Kobs leapt to the same train of thought in redirect examination. "Mr. Melloh, what is the attitude of bishops toward those who disagree as you specified?"

"I'm sure they'd prefer absolute conformity. They themselves won't touch those matters, or if they do, they say those opinions are either sinful or not to be discussed. However, given the great percentage of dissidents in those matters, they have not come down with their historical tactic of excommunication."

"Can smaller groups within the Roman Catholic Church be cults, or cultic to a large degree?"

"It is certainly possible. There are over a billion Catholics. Within that number there are groups, both right and left thinking, who have many cultic characteristics. For example, a dynamic and convincing leader, a zero tolerance for thinking or acting outside the box, etcetera."

"Could the hierarchy as a group fit within the definition of a cult?"

"It's possible."

✠
Chapter Seventeen

"An individual with Narcissistic Personality Disorder, NPD for short, has an array of diagnostic criteria," the witness said in response to Kobs's question. "The DSM-IV, which is the diagnostic manual for psychotherapeutic professionals, lists nine." The psychiatrist, Dr. Ludwig Schmidt, diminutive in size with a trimmed, full beard, sat placidly in the witness chair.

"Dr. Schmidt. Must all nine be present for the disorder to be diagnosed?" Kobs asked.

"No. Generally five or more are sufficient."

"Describe the criteria for the jury, please."

"Since I don't have the manual with me, I'll do my best to paraphrase. First, the narcissist has an exaggerated sense of self-importance. Possessed by this grandiose sense of self, he or she fully expects that superiority to be acknowledged by others."

"Does that exclude persons who give a humble or pious appearance?"

"By no means. They may use a pious exterior as supporting evidence to their self-image of superior holiness."

"In other words, religiosity does not give people immunity from this disorder?"

"That's correct."

"More diagnostic criteria of narcissists please?"

"They have a fantasy life that is loaded with self-images that possess the heights of beauty, wisdom, love, power, success, and the like. Third, they believe themselves to be so special and unique that only persons of equal status can possibly understand them."

"How do you get inside their minds in order to classify them with this disorder?"

"By analysis, of course. But anyone who listens carefully to a person afflicted in this way, will soon hear phrases like "you couldn't possibly understand me unless you walked on my, shall we say, stilts.""

"Other criteria, please."

"Narcissists require huge amounts of admiration. Paradoxically, their self-esteem is very low. They need praise from others to give them a self. And they are very deft at extracting expressions of admiration from others. Next, they feel entitled to special considerations and can be unreasonable in their demands for it. This sense of entitlement, like their grandiosity, their fantasized superiority, their need for admiration, and other qualities, does not depend on any external achievements on their part."

"So, when we find someone fishing for compliments it means we are dealing with a narcissist?"

"Not necessarily. We all fish for compliments. I can recall my mother always finding something wrong with her cooking even though she was, to my thinking, the best cook in the county. At their first taste of her food, anyone at the table would smother her with compliments. That's not what I mean here. My mother had a rational basis for her fishing. She was a good cook. Narcissists fish when there is no basis for compliments other than their felt sense of specialness."

"Could a bishop be a narcissist?"

"Anyone can be a narcissist. In fact, we all start out life as a narcissist. We direct everything toward ourselves. However, most of us outgrow it."

"More criteria please."

"They will use others. Take advantage of them to get what they want or think they deserve. They are also incapable of empathy. They have to direct everything to themselves, their needs."

"So a narcissist would not feel the pain of an abused child?"

"No. Nor anyone else's pain."

"I think that makes seven diagnostic criteria so far. The rest please."

"There is a great deal of envy in the narcissist. They become green at the successes of others and applause given them. They feel any applause is rightfully their own and will downplay the achievements of others. Finally, narcissists frequently display arrogance and disdain for others. They tend to assume a patronizing posture."

"What happens, Doctor, when a narcissist's perfectionist self-image is threatened?"

"That depends. If it's possible to smother the threat before it does damage, they will do that. If the threat is already public, they will respond with denial first, and, then most probably, they will attack the person or persons who pose the threat."

"Would a narcissist attack people who are already victims if they constitute the threat?"

"It would not matter who poses the threat. The narcissist's primary concern and focus is on themselves as being perfect."

"Thank you, Doctor. No further questions at this time."

BEN BAUER

Ben Bauer sat at his office desk with a bottle of wood glue in front of him. He carefully edged the thumbnail of his left hand under an inch-wide sliver of veneer at the desk's edge. Using a toothpick he inserted glue beneath the vagrant piece of wood. He pressed down with his thumb and wiped away oozing glue excess with his free hand. He then set a metal paperweight where his thumb had been. Finally, he replaced the cap on the glue and set it aside.

Marlene, a volunteer office aide, walked into the office carrying a bundle of mail. "You get the lion's share today, Ben," she said. Seeing the glue bottle, her eyes took on a glint of mischief. "If you need to sniff that stuff, you need a vacation."

Ben looked up at the elderly mother of six grown children. He grinned. "Help yourself, Marlene," he said. "Might be good for you. Might cut down on the sass."

She gave a hearty laugh. "Are you kidding? You forget I hold the key to the liquor cabinet. I should downgrade to glue? Here, this will keep you on track." She set the pile of mail in front of him.

"I didn't know there was a key, or a liquor cabinet for that matter." He eyed the stack of mail. "I should thank you? Go away!"

Marlene reached for the glue. "You done with this?"

"Help yourself."

"I'll find a place to store it."

"Uh-huh. Sure!" Ben turned to the mail. He and the staff had set a policy that he would open all mail that was addressed to no specific person or was not obviously an invoice or trash. That way they assured confidentiality to writers of problem-filled messages. He would also open mail that appeared to be official. Most of the mail would go back to Marlene for distribution.

Piece by piece, penning an occasional reply, he worked his way to the bottom of the pile. There lay a large fourteen by twenty-four-inch manila envelope. Ben glanced at the return address. The chancery office. He hefted the package. Do Not Bend stamped in red, front and back. He tried to guess. A poster? No. The chancery doesn't put out posters. Do not cut on the sealed flap. Pull Tab to Open. He pulled the tab and carefully extricated the contents. Two stiff cardboard rectangles sandwiched the main course. He lifted one and there, beaming in full regalia, was Timothy Thompson.

A typed note lay on the portrait, covering the cardinal's midsection and pectoral cross.

> Dear Reverend Father:
>
> Enclosed find a portrait of His Eminence, Cardinal Timothy Thompson. Please see to its framing. We prefer and suggest a frame of gold, though it may be of gilded wood. The portrait should be hung in a highly visible location in your parish church.
>
> We consider this a matter of significant instructional importance. The laity should all be able to recognize His Eminence and give fitting deference should they encounter him.
>
> With sincere fraternal greetings

It was signed by the Moderator of the Archdiocesan Curia.

Ben carried the rest of the mail and the materials from the chancery out to Marlene and handed them to her.

Marlene put the mail to one side and stared at the portrait. She read the chancery letter. "Now isn't that just too precious," she said. "I'll have Pete make the frame. Maybe some tiny flashing lights all around the perimeter."

"Do I detect a bit of sarcasm, Marlene?" Ben asked.

"A lot of sarcasm. Where are we going to hang this?"

"You and the staff surprise me."

"Okay. I'll get it framed."

Entering church for Mass the next morning, Ben chanced to look up. There at the very top of the sanctuary arch was a gilded rectangle, much too high for the recognition of its blurred innards.

✠

Bill Goulding stood at the prosecution table checking his notes. Looking up, he made a final appraisal of the witness and approached the stand. "Dr. Schmidt, you have testified that all of us begin our lives as narcissists. Is that correct?"

"Yes."

"And that most of us work through that disorder and outgrow it. Is that correct?"

"Yes."

"I'm puzzled. Once a person has outgrown it, cast it aside as not consistent with adulthood, is it likely that he or she would reacquire that trait?"

"Not usually, no."

"Is it even possible?"

"Oh, yes. It is more than possible. We see it in our practice."

Goulding paused, wondering if he should drop this line of questioning. Then, "Can you give us examples?"

"Certainly. We see it in many movie stars, for example. As poor as their childhood may have been, and as hard as they may have worked to arrive, once they arrive they can easily get caught up in the applause and adulation. Some come to need that like a drug. They expect it, exaggerate their accomplishments, and look down from their lofty sense of self on the 'little people.' Another example. Some doctors seem to be lured into narcissism by their training and practice. They have trained with corpses, and their practice confronts them with serious disease and patient deaths. They may experience a need to suppress their feelings. That suppression may lead to an incapacity for empathy. They have abilities that can save lives. That experience may lead them to a god-like self-image and progress into full-blown narcissism. It happens."

"You're not saying that all movie stars and all doctors are narcissists, are you?"

"No, not at all. I'm only giving examples of people who left their original, self-centered state and reacquired it again."

"Dr. Schmidt, I'm not a psychotherapist, but I did read the DSM-IV section on narcissism. It says nothing about reacquiring the disease once it is outgrown."

"That's true. You must remember that the DSM-IV is a diagnostic tool. It helps the professional determine the presence of disease, not necessarily its origins. Moreover, the DSM-IV carries the number four precisely because it is constantly undergoing revisions that incorporate evolved understandings of the psychotherapeutic community. As to your comment, there is an increasing number of professionals beginning to speak and write about what they call 'acquired situational narcissism.' And that is what I have described for you."

Goulding turned away from the witness and mused aloud for the jury. "Well, it sounds like so much theory to me. I think we should wait for the consensus that puts acquired narcissism into the DSM-IV before we decide criminal cases on that basis." He turned back to the witness. "Would you agree, Dr. Schmidt?"

"That depends on —"

"Dr. Schmidt," Goulding interrupted, "is it likely that a large group of people, say thousands, would all be narcissists?"

"Well, it is possible, yes."

Goulding's voice carried skepticism. "For example?"

Unflappable at the inference, the witness looked blandly at Goulding. "An elite military force, for example. The members are indoctrinated as being special. They receive praise for their specialness. They wear the insignia of their specialness. They look upon themselves as warriors without peer, and dismiss the regular foot soldier and the enemy as inferior. They acquire a sense of invulnerability so that when they don't measure up, or are shown to be vulnerable by those they dismiss, they often react with violence. They take it out on whoever is at hand, whether it be innocent enemy noncombatants or in prisoner abuse."

"Is it likely that men committed to God, the entire group of bishops, would all be — No, cancel that. No further questions."

Kobs took up the question in redirect. "Do you believe that, as a group, bishops might be narcissists, that they have reacquired the disorder from their indoctrination and their culture?"

"It's possible, but I am not that close to bishops to give a fully informed response. I can say that they do have characteristics analogous to the elite military group I spoke of."

CATHERINE

The hospital room was spacious, finely appointed, and reserved for patients of status. Catherine sat at the window, her attention shifting from the patchwork of skyscrapers outside to the bed where Paddy lay.

The cardinal slept, an oxygen tube stringing from his nose. Another tube dropped to his arm, carrying a mix of medication and hydration. His lips dropped down into a gaping mouth that emitted spasmodic sounds of labored breathing, snorts, and snores.

Catherine relived the fright of his collapse as they left the courtroom, the scream of the ambulance, and her desperate search for a taxi. She felt the stress of waiting alone for hours in the emergency room. Still seeking calm, she opened the Bible she had read at the trial.

The randomly found page was from the Acts of the Apostles. She read the scene where Ananias, at God's direction, restores the sight of the blind Saul. She stopped at the line: "Immediately things like scales fell from his eyes and he regained his sight." I know that experience, she thought. Only last night.

Paddy's boys, the defendants, had come for dinner. She had

served them all cocktails. The meal was a favorite of Paddy: wild pacific salmon, asparagus, a fruit salad, and Chicago rolls. The three bishops left shortly after the meal. Catherine, the kitchen attended to, joined Paddy in the living room.

"I've been thinking, Paddy," she began. "We're likely to be here in Chicago for weeks yet. I've been so worried." She poured her heart out to him, her fears for him and her fears for her future, her dread of possible destitution. "Couldn't you call in an attorney while we're here in Chicago instead of waiting?"

He snapped at her. "I'm tired of that talk, Catherine. Do you ever think about anyone but yourself?"

His words struck her with the force of a miracle, an unhappy miracle. They opened her eyes. The scales fell.

She looked at Paddy now and listened to his breathing. You've been duped, Catherine, she thought. He never loved you. You were important to him, but only for the slave labor and services you gave him, never for yourself. Can you think of one time over all these years where his sole concern wasn't turned on himself?

She recalled the intermittent birthday cards, always signed "His Eminence, Cardinal Brendan O'Connell." There was the time her heart nearly imploded when he brought her roses — only to learn later they were leftovers from a funeral. There were tender and loving words, of course, but always there as a lure to draw her into his sexual gratification.

Breathes there a man with soul so small, she thought, modifying a favorite poem. But, if I'm honest, I am just as guilty as you are. I manufactured excuses for you. I interpreted your actions as caring for me, as loving concern. I was so blind. How can anyone be so blind? Even if you make it back to Arizona, you will have no concern for me. There will be no inheritance. You know that I will be destitute, and it doesn't move you one bit.

I want my scales back! I don't want this miracle! She reached for a tissue on the bedside table and wiped her wet cheeks dry. She looked at the city outside and caught a glimpse of the cathedral's spire. A strategy began to form in her mind. There might still be time.

Chapter Eighteen

JACKSON

Jumpin' Jesus! I can't get it out of my mind. I could see that hard look in Lucy's eyes. I figured, uh-oh, here it comes again. She was gonna tell me to get my butt back to work. I was ready for her. The trial's almost over. Maybe just a couple days, I'd say. She'd go for that. But no —

"Did I ever tell you about the time your good buddy, Father Ron, tried to feel me up?" she asks me.

"What do you mean by that," I says. At first I figured she was just trying some new way to get me away from this trial.

"Just what I said. He grabbed my boob."

"Father Ron wouldn't do that," I says. "I know the guy. He probably brushed your boob with his arm, turning around or something. Happens all the time," I says. I've known Ron all my life. We was in grade school together. Real nice guy. When he got to be a priest, I'd drive wherever he was gonna say Sunday Mass. He's the guy who gave Lucy instructions.

"Well," Lucy says, "what he did was come up behind me, slip his hand under my blouse, and then under my bra, and then squeezed this way and that. You call that an accident?"

"When did this happen?" I asks.

"When I had my last lesson from him."

"And you still went through with the baptism?"

"Yeah. I did it for you. I knew it meant something to you."

One thing I've learned about Lucy, when she says something, she tells it the way it is. She ain't one for bullshit. "How come you didn't tell me?" I asks.

"I took care of it."

"What's that mean?"

"It means I turned around, caught him by surprise, kneed him as hard as I could in the groin."

"Why didn't you tell me?" I says again. I was getting red hot.

"I told him I was going to tell you."

"What'd he say?"

"He said you wouldn't believe me."

"And you believed him?"

"We weren't married yet. I didn't want to lose you."

"Geez, Lucy, I'd a believed you. You ain't never lied to me."

"Well, I was afraid."

Jumpin' Jesus, if Ron could do that? I can't get the picture of it to go away. If Ron was so much crap, these bishops are probably crap too. Why is it some things ain't never real until it gets personal? Why'd I ever come to this crap trial? Jumpin' Jesus, I'm outta here. Ain't no numbers can help these guys.

The witness peered at Kobs through tiny, wire-rimmed spectacles. An emaciated looking, skin-and-bones man, his hair was shorn to his skull, his hands and face weather beaten into tans and wrinkles. "I hold doctorates in both sociology and anthropology from Harvard," he said. "Once my academic studies were completed, I worked in Latin America, where I studied and wrote on the various cultures there. I now teach at the university here."

"How long were you in Latin America?" Kobs asked.

"Forty-two years."

"Thank you, Doctor. You have written extensively on the subject of power, its manner of use and where it is found. Please give us first an understanding of power."

"Yes. Yes. All cultures rely on one or more forms of power. Permit me to break power down into five primary forms. It will help the understanding.

"First there is the power found in history and tradition. This power lodges itself in the substrata of every culture. It underlies consciousness and filtrates upward as it directs customary behavior.

"Next there is the power of brute force. We have all witnessed its usage in the lust to kill — men like Hitler and Idi Amin.

"Third, there is the power of threat and fear. It is allied to force but is strong enough in itself to achieve desired results. It is the threat of loss, whether of life, of soul, or less.

"Fourth is the power of the carrot. Behavioral control is won by enticement. All these good things, wealth, sex, heaven, whatever, will be yours if —

"Last, but highest on the human scale, is the power of trust. It is won by convincing people that one is trustworthy and that what is asked for is in the other's best interest. It is a power that flows, not from compulsion but from invitation. It is present to some extent in tradition."

Kobs stroked his chin. "In your writings, Doctor, you make frequent reference to the influence of the Roman Catholic hierarchy on the various cultures and institutions. Would you please comment on their use of power in the light of the five forms you have just described?"

"Yes. Yes. Of course they rely heavily on the power of tradition. While the tradition is often idealized and romanticized, it is appealed to as legitimizing the hierarchy's claim to command and obedience. Also, hierarchical use of brute force is well known to any student of history. For example in the Inquisition, and in the possession of slaves by the clergy.

"The use of threat to instill fear and obedience is also common. For example, the juridical instrument of excommunication, a cutting off of the offender from inclusion, has been used in matters as minor as attending the theater, reading a particular newspaper, belonging to a particular organization, voting a certain way, almost anything that might be interpreted as thwarting the hierarchical will and interest.

"The carrot too has been employed, but less often. For example it was used in Vatican attempts to lure the recalcitrant Archbishop Lefebvre back to union with Rome. It was also used in an attempt to prevent Bishop James Shannon from leaving the ministry upon his dissent from the Vatican's position on contraception. He was offered various alternative posts."

The witness looked at Kobs expectantly.

"You didn't mention the power of trust," Kobs said.

"No, I did not —"

FABIAN

I should have been assigned to other stories weeks ago. "Stay put," Ralph ordered. "We want the whole story for the record." So here I am. I've listened through all the testimony about monarchy, addiction, cult, narcissism, and, now, power. A fish smells like fish no matter how you cover it up. And this defense has been nothing but one big, smelly, red herring.

Take power. The point is not episcopal power. Every social entity needs power. Even if you admit that some hierarchical uses of power have been either silly or just plain wrong, the mistakes don't make a case.

The real point is faith. The crisis in the Church has been one of faith. Fidelity to the Church is fidelity to God. Our faith goes to and includes the Church's structure. That's the way Jesus set it up, whether we like it or not. And there is no coercion in the Church. You can belong or not. The only person who gets hurt if you don't belong is you. But it is your free choice.

If you choose to belong, there should be no walking through a cafeteria line selecting those parts of the Church you like or feel comfortable with. You accept it all, even if you don't understand some things. You don't say I'll take the pie, but not the broccoli.

I think that defense attorney, Kobs, has taken us down the wrong path with this insanity defense. Instead of defending three bishops, he has succeeded in creating the suspicion that the entire hierarchy is morally off center. Not successfully, in my judgment, but he has raised the question. If these three bishops come up short in their moral judgment, so does the entire episcopacy, with rare exceptions. Kobs is a Catholic, at least ostensibly. This whole defense makes me wonder though. Is Kobs fronting for some conspiracy? I don't see how, but I'll bring up that possibility in my report at five. Helen will love it.

RENEE

Pope John Paul II said freedom must be consistent with the truth of the human person. Ben talked about that. He said that means authority must be exercised in a way equally consistent with that same truth. Ben put it this way. Love of neighbor, per scripture and the wisdom of ages, speaks the truth about the human person.

It is not always easy to know how to love our neighbor, but it is not the love of abstractions or faceless human forms. If I choose war, I must first put a face on an innocent person destined to die by that action, and be able to clearly tell that person, "We will kill you because —" Could anyone convince the victim-to-be? A person can never be faceless collateral damage.

Bishops failed to put a face on each victim of sexual abuse by priests. They did not tell them that "I am keeping Father Abuser at large and he will abuse you because —" They also fail to put a face on each victim of AIDS in Africa, and prove to them they must die because condoms are contrary to the natural law. They are unable to speak individually face-to-face with real homosexuals and explain why "you are intrinsically disordered" and therefore —

Power exercised in the name of authority must also be consistent with the truth about the human person. It is not abstract principle that has priority in the social and moral order. It is the individual person. Each person has the right to have all basic needs attended to, those needs which, when met, will lift persons to a level where they are able to assume responsibility for themselves and for their neighbors. Episcopal authority and power should be ordered to that goal. It has no other purpose.

When bishops hear the laity speak the truth about the human person from their own lived experience, do the bishops listen? Conservatives today see the church's problem as a crisis of faith. That makes it the laity's problem. I see it as a crisis of trust, the hierarchy's problem.

BEN BAUER

Ben spread peanut butter onto toasted whole wheat slices, grabbed a napkin from the counter, and sat at the worn and marred kitchen table. Into his thoughts and halfway through the sandwich, he realized his neglect, got up, and poured a cup of coffee.

Back at the table, he unfolded the morning paper. The headlines drove all thoughts of coffee and food away. He read carefully.

Margie Dunleavy walked in carrying a phone. "That's what you call food?" she asked, "What a miserable looking lunch." Not waiting for an answer, she handed him the phone. "Father Koslowski. Says it's important."

Ben nodded. "Hi, Johnny. I'm just now reading about it." He pointed out the article to Margie. CARDINAL PLACES PARISH TRUSTEES UNDER INTERDICT.

"It simply sucks, Ben," Johnny said. "The interdict was delivered by carrier last night to each of the board members. I have to say, it didn't come as much of a surprise. Negotiations broke off last week." Johnny sounded defeated. "I tried to broker a peace treaty, but His Lordly Eminence, Timothy the First, cardinal of our archdiocese, wouldn't budge on the one really important item — who will own the property?"

"So where does that leave you with Thompson?"

"I got my own very personal letter. I'm directed to leave the parish immediately. The chancery is working on a new assignment for me. Shit, Ben. If you're reading the article, you can see that Thompson is spinning this all his way. He's done his best, blah, blah, blah. He's made every concession he can, blah, blah, blah. He did not want to call on his *legitimate* authority, blah, blah, blah. He has no other alternative left, blah, blah, blah. Shit!"

"How are the trustees taking it, Johnny?"

"They're meeting as we speak. When I left them to make this call, they were composing a reply to Thompson's press release. The TV guys are scheduled to be here this afternoon. If you watched the news this morning, you saw Thompson's hired spinmaker trying to shape Thompson as the victim in all this. Poor, poor Timothy. All hearts should bleed."

"Sounds like you're in for a media shoot-out. Most important, Johnny, what's your own next move?"

"I'm hanging in here with the trustees, Ben. Are you free tonight?

"I'll make it happen."

"Then I'll see you about eight. Would you call Curly and bring him up to date?"

"I will."

"Thanks. See you at eight. Have bourbon!"

"Will do, Johnny. Good luck."

Margie set the paper on the table. "So that's what an interdict is," she said. "They're guilty of causing scandal by inviting others to disobedience. For that they are forbidden the sacraments." She looked at Ben. "Since when is calling a thief a thief inciting others to disobedience?"

Ben, suddenly depressed by a feeling of helplessness, lifted his hands palms up. "They make a law that gives them the authority to be thieves, Margie, just not in those words."

"Thieves!" Margie threw up her hands and walked out.

Chapter Nineteen

JUDGE MONROE

Monroe's spindly face and black-robed shoulders barely rose above the bench. She turned her piercing black eyes toward the jury. "Members of the jury," she began, "now that you have seen and heard evidence and arguments from both prosecution and defense, I will instruct you on the law. I have decided to give you this instruction prior to the closing arguments so that you might bring the information into your understanding of those arguments.

"As a jury you have two responsibilities. First, you must decide the facts from the evidence presented to you. Second, you must apply the law that I give you.

"I ask that you perform these duties fairly and without partiality. Neither public opinion, fear, nor sympathy should influence you. You should use your own common sense in your considerations. You may draw conclusions from inference as we often do in daily life. By that I mean we often clearly see one fact and conclude another from the first.

"Even though three defendants are on trial here, you must give separate consideration to each of them.

"To sustain the charge of conspiracy, the government must prove there was an agreement among the defendants to protect sexual abusers. If you find that this has not been proven beyond a reasonable doubt, you should find the defendants not guilty.

"If you decide they are guilty beyond reasonable doubt, and that the defense has proven by convincing evidence that they were insane at the time of their felonious actions, you should find them not guilty only by reason of insanity.

"As a general rule, the law understands insanity to mean that defendants at the time of their crime were unable to distinguish right from wrong, or that a mental disease made them unable to control their actions even though they knew their actions to be wrong.

"Upon retiring to the jury room, you will select one of you to act as foreperson. The foreperson will . . .

"Should you need to contact me for any reason during your deliberations, you will do so in writing.

"When you have reached a verdict by unanimous agreement, the-foreperson will . . ."

PROSECUTION

"Ladies and gentlemen of the jury!" Bill Goulding stood erect and confident in front of the jury box, his classic profile to the audience. "Do you remember the old shell game? The pitchman has three walnut half-shells set on a small table. He holds a pea in his hand and puts it under one of the shells. 'Watch the shells,' he says. 'That's all you have to do. Know where that pea is and you win.' Then he begins to switch the shells round and round, the pea drops unnoticed in his palm. You're sure you know which walnut hides the pea. He lifts the walnut. The pea is not there. You are amazed, and you are a loser. Never buy into a shell game. You will always lose.

"The defense has been trying to direct your attention away from the incontrovertible fact that these grown men, these defendants, leaders in their Church, accepted arbiters of right and wrong, have committed the felonies as charged. They want to shift your attention from the fact of guilt to speculation on *why* the defendants are guilty. They are guilty. The defense passively admitted the guilt when they changed to a plea of mental defect. At that moment the defense made this a trial of the *why* of guilt. Keep your eye on the guilt, not on the shell movements of the defense.

"Mr. Kobs would have you believe that these defendants could not have acted otherwise, that they are trapped by some heretofore unknown and unnamed mental disease akin to, but not exactly like, addiction and narcissism — and all the rest of his nonsense. He proposes that they are crazed with power and their minds have been captured by a cult-like social structure. Ladies and gentlemen, it is all baloney. It is all a contrivance in the mind of the defense attorney for the sole purpose of planting doubt in your minds, of distracting you with a shell game, and seducing you from your own common sense. It's a shell game!

"Don't believe it! If these bishops didn't know their protection of pedophiles was criminal, why did they try to conceal it? If they didn't experience guilt, there was no need to hide."

Goulding paused and looked from juror to juror. "Think, ladies and gentlemen, think instead of the crimes those priest pedophiles committed, were able to commit, because they were protected by these defendants. They were assigned over and over again to parishes where innocent children waited and trusted. Think of the abused children, children like your own, or those close to you. Think of the sodomy, the rapes, the suicides, the destruction of a future for so many. These defendants could have prevented it all. Instead they aided and abetted both the predators and each other.

"If the defense is correct, ladies and gentlemen, how many corporate leaders must we find innocent by reason of insanity because their corporate cultures permitted abuses like the plundering of retirements from thousands and every other sort of felonious abuse?

"Could we indeed find any criminal act criminal if a society or its culture can be blamed? No, ladies and gentlemen, draw a line in the sands of justice. Hold these men accountable because they are accountable."

FABIAN

It's a reporter's greatest nightmare, having one's boss sit next to you for a story's finale.

"I'm not going to tell you how to write it," she says. "I'm here to observe."

Don't you believe it. Her observing has been a never-ending string of questions.

"Did Kobs ever say anything at all to tie all this addiction and cult blarney specifically to the three defendants?" Helen whispers.

"No."

"So, he *is* out to hang the entire hierarchy?"

Helen likes to put oomph into *is* and *are*. It's her way of doing bullet points. "Looks that way to me. He wants to get the defendants off by linking them to some moral malaise shared by the whole bunch."

"If that's his tactic, those three bishops allowed him to do it. They had to buy into the mental defect plea," Helen says. "Stupid! How could they be that stupid? If they had any balls they would have gone down with their own ship."

Helen likes to use the word *balls*. "Can't blame them," I answer. "They probably didn't see where Kobs would take their plea. To tell the truth, I didn't see it coming. I doubt if anyone in the courtroom, including Judge Monroe, saw it. My own suspicions didn't start until halfway through the defense."

"Secular humanists have no conscience. They're anarchists. They tear down, but don't have a clue where to go after the havoc. I wonder how they got to Kobs. You *are* going to write this as a conspiracy, aren't you?"

"No," I say. "I haven't found a conspiracy. Only a damn clever defense tactic. I think it might even succeed. If their faces tell the story, the jury has been impressed by the defense. They hang on every twist Kobs gives the testimony."

"Bah!"

Bah is Helen's favorite claim to victory in disputation.

DEFENSE

Kobs stood centered in front of the jury box, an imposing figure. His eyes moved across the members' faces. His demeanor thoughtful, his right hand moved once, a smoothing stroke down across his red stubble beard.

"Ladies and gentlemen of the jury. You have witnessed the testimonies that depict the privileged lives of bishops. You have seen their mimicking of aristocracy and royalty in their purple culture. They plead humility and poverty, but their lives display the opposite. It is true to say that, like their monarchical counterparts down through history, they have raised perfumed handkerchiefs to their noses to avoid the gangrenous odor that goes with sexual abuse of children.

"You have listened to the testimony on addiction and heard how neatly that disease fits the relationship between bishops and their culture of self-interest. You have seen how symptoms like denial, perfectionism, and personal exemptions to normal standards of morality are visible in their conduct.

"You have seen and heard how the episcopal culture approximates the culture of cult, and how the centering on a single figure, the pope, defines that culture. They claim infallibility through the papacy, but their own history drives that claim into question.

"Through the testimony of experts, you have seen the narcissistic qualities of their culture. Those qualities are exhibited over the entire spectrum of their behavior, but perhaps no more strongly than in their exercise of power. Force, self-serving traditions, threat, fear, carrot. That is the order of exercise. It is a moral axiom that love of neighbor reigns at the apex of the moral order. That is what moral leaders should be about. Love establishes an order in which trust is an essential component. One does not experience trust either within or extending from the purple culture. It is a power left to rust in their armory.

"Mr. Goulding has posed the question, why did they conceal their abetment of sexual abusers if they did not experience guilt from doing so? He suggests it proves their accountability. Ladies and gentlemen, they did not experience guilt because their addiction to the purple culture blinded them to the devastation. They did not experience guilt because they were able to give themselves a personal exemption from wrongdoing. They did not experience guilt because it would question their perfectionism. They did not experience guilt because they were so conditioned by their unique and purple culture."

RENEE

This trial should adjourn for lunch any minute. Last week Ben invited me to join a group of his friends that get together once a month. Last night was the first time I met with them. There were sixteen of us, a mix of lay people, nuns, and priests. I could tell how close they were when Ben began sharing his innermost thoughts and feelings. He's usually emotionally up, transforming whatever might be unpleasant into a joke, but last night he was down. He told the group that the only thing wrong with the Church is the leadership. Until then I've never heard him utter a callous word.

"They are Scott Peck's people of the lie," he said. "From where I am positioned in this Catholic universe, I see them operating, unconsciously perhaps, from the malignant narcissism Peck writes of."

That's the first time Ben has given me that intimate a glimpse into the pain he goes through.

"If I stay, am I not participating in their lie?" he asked us. "If I leave the ministry, will I not be abandoning my people to the hierarchical lie?"

He says the entire hierarchy is on trial here, not just the three bishops. Kobs's defense makes sense to Ben, but I'm still conflicted.

DEFENSE

"Members of the jury," Kobs continued, "the purple culture is like a castle fortress, full of nooks and crannies, towers and dungeons. It has a benign exterior appearance and projects no visible fearsome threat. We associate castles today with fairy princesses and tales of brave and grandiose knightly quests. But, ladies and gentlemen, in the castle of the purple culture, self-interest has found a home in those nooks and crannies, towers and dungeons. Tucked away in every crevice are scrolls of customs and laws that legitimize the use of any means to defend against any perceived threat to the purple culture. The inhabitants of this culture are authorized to do harm to others with the God-approved intention of service to the culture. Isn't that insane?

"Episcopal behavior exhibits many more symptoms of their moral malaise. As we have learned here from expert testimony, addicts need to control whatever might threaten their addiction. Bishops exhibit this need to control. We have seen their attempts to control a widespread cover-up of sexual abuse by their priests, which they viewed as a giant threat to their culture. Ladies and gentlemen, are we dealing with moral sanity here?

"Another symptom: bishops have given themselves to a gospel

message of being servants to every neighbor. But then they live in a style where every neighbor is made servant to their grandiosity. Isn't that an over-the-top bit of narcissism?

"Yet another symptom: the literature of the hierarchy is full of recognition for the presence of the Holy Spirit in the people at large. But when the people attempt to share the wisdom they have learned from their spirit-filled experience, they are treated with contempt. For example, think of how they treat parents whose lives are given to the service of life, a home full of children, but who also know that their sexuality is equally given to the service of love. They know when enough is enough. But do the bishops listen to the people's message about contraception? No!

"How about another symptom: bishops proclaim the full equality of women. Have you ever seen a woman priest, bishop, or cardinal? No. Women would threaten their purple culture."

Kobs raised his eyes toward the ceiling and mused *Control. Control. Control.*

"How many symptoms should I give? The hierarchy proclaims the dignity and equality of all people, but continue their royal fantasies by the investitures of knights, dames, and ladies. Members of the jury, you must remember that aristocracy relates only to aristocracy. Can you detect narcissism in all that?

"One more symptom and I'll stop, though the list goes on. We are back to their need for control. Bishops feel compelled to control the very thinking of their people. They require that experts, invited to speak within their boundaries, be subject to prior episcopal approval. Bishops are unwilling or unable to respond to challenge with open debate. We see this clearly in their furtive silencing of theologians, and their behind-the-scenes maneuvers to fire editors who practice openness to all voices. Just think of it. If any organization ought to be the exemplar of openness, clarity, and fairness, wouldn't you expect the hierarchy to be that organization?

"Ladies and gentlemen, how many symptoms do we need to *see* before we *see* disease?

JACOB

Inez and Deenah stopped coming to the trial last week. I suspect that all of Deenah's questions have been answered, and that Inez knows that I am tranquil about it now. Deenah's interest lagged after that Father Dan's arrest. The two of them are at the art museum today or shopping.

I'm glad I stayed with it. When Dad pulled us all out of the Catholic Church, I hadn't even been introduced to a catechism yet. So Kobs's defense and all the expert testimony have helped me understand Dad better.

What a terrible weight these bishops are on their laity. They should be lifting people up, helping them carry their already heavy burdens. Instead, they sit on them. I feel so free compared to my Catholic friends.

That these defendants suffer from a mental defect rings true. At least it is consistent with Dad's decisions. I know what my verdict would be, but I'm sure the jurors are weighing the evidence carefully. I doubt, though, if they bring the same experiences to their decision making that I would.

If they find for mental defect, I can't imagine what kind of treatment facility the judge will decide on. What kind of treatment could possible be effective for these men — really for the entire hierarchical institution with its closed culture? I must say that purple says it all to me. But how do you erase purple?

DEFENSE

"Ladies and gentlemen," Kobs said, "bishops are helpless against their past. They have been cultured in a petri dish where the controlled medium is the purpled past. They emerge an opaque purple that sees only the past and disrupts their unique moral orientation. They are compelled to set course by a moral compass that has fallen off point.

"They are left with no mental space to reexamine the past because they see that past as glorious and golden. They have no room to listen to the present, to take a different course, no room to consider the gospel's egalitarian future.

"They live in a closed culture, a closed society which in their purpled vision is a perfect society. Since they *are* the society *they* are perfect. My friends, you cannot beat perfect. There is no comparative for perfect, no perfecter or more perfect. Neither is there a superlative for perfect, no perfectest or most perfect. Perfect cannot be improved, so there is no need for change. We have seen how callously they deal with any slight to that image of perfection. They see themselves as morally covered by a personal and purple exemption.

"The prosecutor, Mr. Goulding, would have you believe that if the hierarchical culture is morally defective because of mental defect, we would be obliged to exonerate any villainous corporate CEO on the same basis. My friends, there is no parallel between the two cultures. We do not look to the corporate world for moral leadership. We expect it of bishops. CEOs can be fired and replaced at the demand of shareholders. The laity has no voice in the hiring or firing of bishops. Corporate cultures can be challenged and changed — overnight. Not so the purple culture. Corporate cultures are oriented to the future, to customers and to profit. The purple culture is oriented inward and to the past.

"Ladies and gentlemen, I cannot prove to you that these defendants suffer from a mental defect. Neither can Mr. Goulding prove to you that these men acted out of either ignorance or evil. It is for you to decide, and your decision determines their fate.

"You cannot believe that these men acted out of ignorance. Look at their education and their advanced degrees.

"Nor can you believe that these defendants are consciously and maliciously evil. They simply don't see us, or hear us, or smell our sweat, or feel our feelings. If they touch us, it is covertly done in self-interest. Their senses have been dulled by a purple drug. That's what cultures of royalty, addiction, narcissism, and cult all have in common.

"Ladies and gentlemen, mental defect is the most logical explanation for how these men, dedicated to the Christian gospels, could fail in their moral responsibility. They simply could not see the faces of victims abused by their subordinate clergy. It is a tragic indictment of them and of the culture that spawned them.

"Only outside intervention can cure them of their disease. The same is true of addiction and of cult membership. I do not personally know the cure for royal pretenses and for narcissism, nor do I have a name for this hierarchical disease. Purple Narcissism might suffice. Psychologists might not locate this disease because it is not specifically in their catalogue. You can put it there.

"Members of the jury, if you suddenly discovered a culture isolated in remote mountain enclaves, and the priests of that culture practiced human sacrifice, what would you do? Stop the practice, of course! But, would you imprison them for their beliefs. I don't think so. You would have them reoriented into the world of our moral values.

"So, is the sexual abuse of children very different from human sacrifice? Would you put these bishops in jail to satisfy justice, or would you commit them to another sort of petri dish to leach away the purple and reculture them so that their moral compass points once again to humankind's true North? Members of the jury, I suggest that real justice and the best interest of all your neighbors comes down on the side of the petri dish."

Kobs turned to the bench. "The defense rests, Your Honor."

✠

Chapter Twenty

MARCIE AND DAVID

Marcie and David dropped briefcases into a vacant booth at The Corner Pub, a much frequented lunch site for young professionals. They were jubilant. The call from the courthouse had come at ten thirty a.m. The jury would announce its decision at eleven. It took them twenty minutes to find Kobs, but all three took their seats at the defense table with the bishops just as the jury members were filing in.

The jury foremen repeated the verdict for each defendant by name. For each: "Not guilty only by reason of insanity." Barieno sat stone-faced. Sandes lowered, then closed his eyes. Courteer winced, grimacing, his eyes moist.

"He did it again," Marcie exclaimed. She signaled a waiter. This calls for a celebration.

"Reisling," she said. "David?"

"Miller draft," David said to the waiter. He looked at Marcie. "It's been a while since we drank on the job."

"We've never had a case like this or a victory like this," she replied.

The waiter returned with their beverages. "Caesar salad," Marcie directed. "David?"

"Cheeseburger and fries."

When the waiter left, Marcie raised her glass to David. "To the boss! He absolutely nailed it with the purple culture defense."

They clicked glasses.

"And here's to the verdict," David exclaimed and raised his glass to Marcie's.

Marcie sipped her wine. "Just before we left the courthouse, Jim was talking with the bishops. I was getting my gear together. Did you hear what he said to them?" she asked.

"I did. He said something like, 'Well, gentlemen, we've done our best for you, and succeeded to the extent that success was possible. Your future is now in your hands.'"

"Even so, the verdict didn't seem to please the bishops that much. They looked pretty glum."

"Maybe insight is dawning," David said as their orders arrived.

Marcie raked through lettuce in search of chicken chunks. "The jury took three full days of deliberation," she mused. "Did you expect it to take that long?"

"I expected it would take longer since they requested another look at all of the testimony from the defense's witnesses, none from the prosecution. To me, that says they had no question as to guilt, but wanted to be sure they fully understood Jim's argument."

"The perfect judge, a perfect jury," Marcie said. "What happens to the bishops now? I suppose they get sent to some sort of treatment facility, but what sort? I'm not familiar with any facility with expertise to take aristocracy out of aristocrats or to change purple into the various hues of humanity."

"I'm sure Judge Monroe has staff scrambling on that question," David replied.

Between bites, Marcie asked, "David, do you ever wonder about the people who attended the trial?"

"What about the people?"

"Why were they there? Were they simply curious? Was it something personal? How the jury decision affected them?"

"Any people in particular?"

"I don't know their names, but like that man who had the outburst in court, accusing Bishop Barieno of abusing his son; like that lady who was always by the cardinal's side. Was she connected to the trial or just to the cardinal? Like that beautiful young lady who sat with the elderly couple up front. Don't tell me you didn't notice her, David. Do you suppose she was a victim? Or like that reporter for *True Catholic.* I had a chat with him in the hall one afternoon. I wonder about people like that."

"I do wonder about the relationship between Jim and Goulding," David said. "I know they're personal friends and socialize, so I wonder if the trial outcome affects that, and how."

ROELLY

Mary Roelly poured coffee for her husband, Mike, returned the pot to the coffeemaker, and sat opposite him at the kitchen table. "Eat your eggs before they get cold, Mike," she said softly.

Mike, his eyes busy scanning the front page of the morning newspaper, did as she suggested. He placed the open paper next to his plate, picked up his fork, and took a bite. He continued to read and turned to the second page. "Here it is, Mary," he said suddenly, and then added, "finally." He read aloud:

> Bishop Charged with Sexual Abuse of Minors
> Only one day after his trial for conspiracy to protect priest sexual abusers of children ended, Bishop Vincent Barieno of Palm Springs, Florida, was himself charged with sexually abusing young

boys when he was pastor of St. Sebastian parish here in the city more than a decade ago.

The charge was made possible because Barieno has been out of the state for nearly ten years and that period of time does not count when computing whether the statute of limitations has expired. It has not.

The investigation of Barieno began with an outburst in court during the conspiracy trial, reported in this newspaper, when Michael Roelly accused Barieno of molesting his son. The young man had committed suicide only days before. Mr. Roelly's claim led to revelations and accusations from other men who alleged that Barieno had sexually abused them also.

Reports from sources within the District Attorney's Office, but as yet unverified as we go to press, say that Barieno has pled guilty. He is scheduled for arraignment in court tomorrow. We are informed that the pleas of guilty will be made at that time.

Mike looked up. There were tears in Mary's eyes. He got up, helped her to stand, and wrapped her in his arms. "It's over, Mary. We've got to remember that Paul died thinking we could then be happy. We owe it to him to work ourselves up to happiness. He'll be waiting to greet us up there, and we'll want to tell him we did our best for happiness." He wiped at her tears with his fingers.

CATHERINE

Catherine sat alone in the chancery reception waiting area. "The cardinal could grant you a few minutes," the receptionist said, after checking with his secretary. Catherine watched the receptionist's lips as, headset in place, she responded to calls.

Paddy's death was still a vivid memory. He had been in the hospital for nearly a week when the doctors released him with severe restrictions on his physical activity. When the doctors had left the room, Catherine brought Paddy's clothes from the closet and set them at the foot of his bed. She then moved to his side and took his hands to help him sit up. Suddenly his mouth gaped and his eyes filled with surprise. He became deadweight and fell back. In death his eyes remained open, staring. He's registering disbelief, she had thought.

Nurses and doctors rushed at her call. There was nothing they could do. She stayed with his body until the funeral home personnel came for it. From that moment, after all those years, he was out of her care and in the cold hands of his peers. The line for the viewing wound for blocks from the cathedral. She had joined the line, but left after an hour, still hours from the coffin. She was not invited to the funeral, but went anyway. She'd found a corner in the choir loft. The eulogies went on and on, stocked with over-used clichés, none of them revealing the true Brendan Patrick O'Connell.

"His Eminence will see you now, Catherine." The cardinal's secretary had been an acquaintance from the old days. She ushered Catherine to the office and opened the door.

Cardinal Thompson was at his best, expansive and gracious. He ushered Catherine to a seat in a corner appointed as a conversational area. He took a seat across from Catherine, looked at his watch, and smiled sympathy at her. "It must be a very difficult time for you," he said.

"It is."

"Is there anything I can do?"

"Cardinal O'Connell promised me that he would care for my old age. It appears that he neglected to do that."

"I see." Thompson made sympathy sounds. "Mmmm, I'm sure

we can find something for you, Catherine. There must be house-keeper openings in the archdiocese."

"But that's not what Paddy, I mean Cardinal O'Connell, prom-ised me."

The sympathy tone began to leave Thompson's voice. "Of course, as you said yourself, Catherine. We have no record of what His Eminence intended in your regard. I'm afraid that fact ties my hands as far as supporting you with archdiocesan monies."

"You were a friend of his, weren't you?" Catherine asked.

"Yes, I was. He was a great man and very helpful to me."

"You would know his voice if you heard it?"

"Yes, of course. The world would recognize his voice. So vibrant and unique."

Catherine pulled a small CD player and earphones from her purse. "Please listen to this, Your Eminence." She handed him the equipment.

Thompson demurred. He looked at his watch. "I truly don't have time —"

"Listen to his words," she said, a hint of warning in her voice.

Thompson put the headset on and punched the play button.

Catherine sat back and watched his expression. He was listening to Paddy reminisce about his sexual prowess with her as she led him through a series of special memories that covered their time together.

Thompson listened for perhaps twenty minutes. He stared at Catherine. His tone took on a hint of a supplicant. "Catherine, you know that we can't have this made public. The scandal would rever-berate throughout the world. It would do great damage and defame the memory of a cardinal of the Church."

"I know." She reached for the headset.

"What exactly is it that you want?" Thompson was wary.

Catherine knew that she had the best hand and that he knew she knew. She withdrew a folded sheet from her purse and handed it to

Thompson. She also handed him a business card. "My attorney," she said, rising.

Thompson scanned the paper. "This is too much," he said. "Couldn't we come to —"

"No. That's it. It's fair and you know it. It was promised to me, and my conscience is clear. Your attorneys can see my attorney. When the deal is signed, you get the original CD. She stood. "Thank you for your time, Your Eminence." She walked out.

A smile warmed her face as she walked along the avenue. She knew he'd pay: Paddy's apartment tax free for life, a substantial monthly stipend tied to inflation, and a half million to see her through any old-age illnesses. She walked a brisk, carefree pace.

JACOB

Jacob pulled the hose to the back lot line where a six-foot-wide blaze of blooms ran the length of the property. As he sprayed the flowers, he listened to the sounds coming from Inez and Deenah, who were hatching plans at the patio table. Giggles and whoops punctuated their conversation, unintelligible at this distance.

He wondered at the depth of their intimacy and how it could come to be so rapidly. When he didn't understand some facet of human relations, Inez had always provided the wisdom. Now he credited their closeness to Deenah to Inez's magical instincts. Deenah was living with them now, and he marveled at her development from a tentative overall posture to a bright confidence. Inez again. Glancing in their direction, his eye caught the movement of the postal van pulling to the curb. He turned off the hose and went to retrieve the mail.

Junk, junk, letter for Inez, junk, bill, bill, junk, letter for Deenah, bill he recited to himself shuffling through the stack. He delivered the pile to the patio table.

Inez poured him a glass of lemonade, took the mail, and sorted. "Deenah, it's from Northwestern University," she said, handing a letter to the girl.

Jacob sensed a sudden tension in the women as Deenah opened the letter with the jackknife he provided. She read and exclaimed, "I've been accepted."

Both women were on their feet shrieking and hugging. Jacob stood and joined the hugging. He wasn't a whooper.

"Deenah and I were talking," Inez said, "if she was accepted she would continue to live here with us and commute — at least for the first year. Oh my, there's so much to do. Shopping to be done, school supplies, clothes." The two women became fully engaged in plans.

Jacob returned to the hose. As the spray flowed, his mind also turned to planning. They would make a study area for Deenah in their second-story library where he and Inez already had desks. Plenty of room. Her desk can go by the window looking back at these flowers. She'll need a computer. We'll get the desk, chair, and computer this week. She'll need a car for her daily commute. She doesn't drive so that means instructions, license — lots to do.

He looked at the flowers. Paradise, he thought. Life has become a paradise. Joy and beauty out of pain and rubble. I'm near to bursting.

FABIAN

I love this old pressroom, and a steaming cup of coffee, and my cubicle, and the sound of presses running on the floor below. I do not love the place to which I have been summoned, Helen's office one floor up.

Helen obtained a copy of the trial transcript and has spent days going through it. She thinks I missed something, Frank says. He'll be at the meeting, thank God. It's like going to the dentist with the sure knowledge he'll find a deep-seated cavity. All you can imagine is the whirr of the drill — and pain. It's time. Oh, what the hell, Fabian, get your butt up there. Don't forget your coffee.

Upstairs I knock on her door and get a "come in."

"Morning, Helen, morning, Frank."

They respond in kind.

"Let's get right to it," Helen says.

"Fine," I say. "Any problem?"

Helen takes off on Kobs's defense. She is livid. After listening a while, I find that her gripe isn't what Kobs did to the hierarchy. She is pissed over the heraldry testimony and how Kobs used it.

"What's wrong with knights?" she says, being rhetorical. "My Harold is a Knight Commander of the Order of St. Gregory." She softened a little. "You've both seen him in uniform — so handsome! Breathtaking! Truly noble!"

I have seen Harold in his uniform. He reminded me of a rotund Jackie Gleason in the *Honeymooners* dressed in the official uniform of the Raccoon Lodge. Harold bulged. One of those raccoon hats with tail attached might have drawn attention to it and improved Harold's looks. Better yet, the bulges might have gone unnoticed had he let loose with the Raccoon's greeting: Ooo-Wooo!

"And I'm a Dame of the Order of St. Gregory," Helen went on, her voice rising. "And let me tell you this. Harold and I paid our dues to get those titles. How dare this common guttersnipe Kobs make light of, no make that *ridicule,* all the heraldry and traditions of the aristocracy. It's low despicable people like Kobs who are responsible for class unrest."

I raise my hands in a what-can-I-say gesture.

By now she is tight-lipped. "The papal nuncio and the cardinal have asked me to bury any comment on the trial." She looks at Frank. "Scrub the conspiracy article! They both said they will not support an appeal of the verdict," she added. "They want to let the matter die as quickly as possible, so we will cooperate and print nothing more about the trial. I think they're hoping for some sort of natural disaster to switch people's attention. Between us, I don't think they have the balls for a good fight."

I'm thinking I wouldn't take Frank's editor job for all the gold of a cardinal's trinkets.

"As for you, Fabian," she says, eyeing me sternly. "If you ever see the names of Kobs or Goulding in any context, I want to be informed. Understand? I'm not going to forget this. If they ever attack the Church again I'll be on them like a tiger."

I nod.

"Okay, get hopping," she says.

Next to *balls*, Helen's favorite words are *get hopping*.

RENEE

Renee listened with a phone at her ear. "Yes, I understand. Thank you very much. I'll be there at ten on Monday. That's wonderful news. I'm excited. Thank you again. Good-bye."

Placing the phone in its cradle, she gave a cheerleader's jump with arms outstretched. "Yes! Yes!" she shouted. You're a working girl again, Renee. You've got your university job. Yes, she thought. I've got to call Ben.

She dialed. "Ben, I just got the word. I've been hired at the university. An associate professor job. I just had to tell you."

"Great news, Renee," Ben replied with enthusiasm. "We should celebrate. I'll call a special meeting of our group. We've got two things to celebrate. Your job and the results of the trial. We're all in need of some good news. I'll check with everybody and get back to you with a date. Thanks for brightening my day."

Ben called Renee back that same afternoon. "It's all set up. We'll have it at the rectory tomorrow evening at six. Everybody's bringing something. I get to cook my speciality, really gourmet. I'm thinking something at the top of my culinary skills: wieners, potato buds, and Bavarian-style sauerkraut. Margie is bringing a cake. How does that sound?"

"Sounds perfect. What can I bring?"

"How about something to drink?"

"I can bring wine. Or should that be beer?"

"Beer, I think. Don't you?"

"Light or dark?"

"I would guess light. You know, with wieners?

"Done. Is everyone coming?"

"They wouldn't miss it for anything short of a blizzard."

Renee hung up the phone, a feeling of well-being flooding her body. Life is good, she thought. No, life is shades of wonderful. Now go get the beer, Renee.

KOBS AND GOULDING

Bill Goulding and Jim Kobs watched the sun turn the morning lake into dazzle as the captain brought the fishing boat toward the dock at Bailey's Harbor. Their day and quest for salmon had begun at four a.m. On land they headed straight to the local beanery for breakfast. The skipper would see that the catch was cleaned and the filets frozen.

"I thank you in advance for buying breakfast," Goulding said, beginning the banter.

"What do you mean? You're buying," Kobs responded.

"Most fish was the bet. Or don't you remember?"

"I remember."

"You don't seem to remember that I caught six salmon. You caught four."

"That's right," Kobs said. "But my four weighed in at forty-eight pounds. Your six weighed only forty-four. I caught the most fish."

"Don't give me that malarkey. When it comes to fish, 'most' has to do with numbers. Always has. Always will."

Both men were enjoying the exchange.

"What are you, a lawyer or something?" Kobs asked. And then gave in. "Okay, I'll buy, but I may appeal."

"Appeal away." The waiter arrived, poured coffee and took their order. "I'll have the eggs, bacon, and pancakes. He'll have the bill," Goulding said.

"We told Celina and Jeanne to pick us up at ten. They'll be shopping for another hour, so we've got some time to talk," Kobs said. "You know, Bill, Guggenbuhl is retiring completely from practice at the end of the month. The job is yours if you'll take it. Full partnership, equal split of the income, all the bennies. If I'm guessing right that should quadruple your present take. What with three kids in college, the job could be helpful. I've talked to Sam Mayer. He's completely on board with it. We'd both like to have you as a partner. You're a terrific prosecutor. We think you'd enjoy the defense side."

"Well, first of all, I appreciate the offer, Jim. I like what I'm doing, but your offer is very tempting. I'll talk to Jeanne. The main problem I see is that I wouldn't be able to engage you in battle in the courtroom anymore."

"We can work on that. Maybe some sort of after-the-fact armchair quarterback talk."

The restaurant that evening had the aura of dusk in its lighting. The white tablecloth sparkled with polished silverware in soft candlelight. The two men seated their wives, sat, and ordered wine. For a time they were all silent, enjoying the view of the bay, still glinting in the early evening sun. A waiter filled their water glasses and the wine steward arrived with their wine.

"Remember your promise," Celina said. "No talking shop."

"None means none," Jeanne added.

"We remember," they chimed.

"We hashed the trial over completely this morning," Bill said. "Allow me only one more comment and I'll not mention the trial again." Turning to Jim, "This is the first time in my experience that the defense has wrested the task of prosecution from the prosecutor. I think, on reflection, justice was better served." He raised his glass. "Cheers."

LILLITH

Lilith drove her rented car off the county highway onto Federal Road and was quickly met by a large sign. An arrow above the words WAR-DEN STATE HOSPITAL with a subtitle WARDS FOR THE CRIMINALLY INSANE pointed left. Pointing right, an arrow indicated Warden Federal Prison. She turned left and pulled up to the gate, where an armed correction officer exited a guard station, hand on holster, and approached her driver's-side window.

The officer was polite, but all business. He asked the purpose of her visit, examined her identification, and the contents of the back seat and trunk. Only then did he signal another officer to open the gate. She drove through and pulled into a visitor parking space.

At the main entrance she again went through an interrogation, had her credentials examined, and was sent through a metal detector. An officer then led her down a long hall and through a heavy glass door. There she was seated facing an opening much like an old-time bank cashier's window set in a barred enclosure. The officer left the room. She heard the lock click and turned to see the officer standing watchfully on the other side of the door.

Robert appeared through the opening. She winced at the sight of his pained features, visible as he sat down. Sensing his embarrassment, she began an awkward search for words, then asked tenderly, "How are you, Robert?"

Robert's eyes told the story. They were hazed and vacant, the man lost behind their emptiness. He gave a little shrug.

"Are you comfortable, Robert?" she asked.

"I guess." He was hesitant. "You've always said that I'm a hermit, Lilith. I am. I'd be comfortable in a monk's cell. So I guess I'm comfortable." He paused. "But I also realize here that I've been able to be a hermit because I had the support of others. Specifically, your support, Lillith. You saw to food, to shelter, to all the amenities. I am not the live-in-a-cave type of hermit. I have support here for food and shelter, but —"

"But what, Robert?"

"But I'm not free to get up and go to the library or to the garden or anywhere. I do not have someone sit across from me at table and challenge me as you did. I find that I'm a hermit who needs companionship. How is that for an oxymoron?"

"Not an oxymoron, Robert, but a breakthrough! No one can live and grow as a hermit. We all need others."

"Do you think so?" he said absently. "They tell me I'm scheduled for some sort of evaluation, but not for two more weeks. The psychiatrists are waiting for a trial summation and guidance from Judge Monroe. It all seems so inefficient."

"You've moved from one authoritarian culture where you were the authority to another where you are a subject. That experience also might provide insight if you consider it carefully."

"You talk of breakthroughs and insights. My faith goes to everything Catholic, and I mean everything. It goes to the dogma, the moral norms, the canon laws, the regulations for ritual, the hierarchical structure, all the devout practices, to everything, Lilith. The thought of searching for a breach in that solid wall of faith frightens me beyond words. Would I not have abandoned God if I abandon even a tiny part? If I even question anything?"

"I think that conscience requires that we are ever-questioning, Robert."

"You do? If you were in my place looking at this seamless wall of faith, where would you begin? Can you suggest some point of particular weakness where the wall might be breached?"

"Well, you might begin with the fiocchi Attorney Kobs said are symbolic of the purple culture. Try and place all elements of that culture over against the gospels and permit the inconsistencies to enter your mind."

"You think the purple culture is an accurate representation?"

"I do."

"You'll support me through this, won't you, Lilith?"

"Of course I will. I will be here every week. I can bring you books if it is permitted."

"Can you suggest any other points of weakness in my shield of faith?"

"I'll reflect on that. The moral norms you mentioned come to mind. Why is there no recognition among your peers of changes over the centuries that are diametrically opposed to positions once held? I'm thinking of usury, slavery, democracy, religious freedom. And there are more. You know your history, Robert. Try placing those changes over against your unexamined presumption of inerrancy and infallibility. See if that shakes your cultural assumptions."

"Even if that does change me, what do I do then?"

"You try to change your peers. They should be here with you and Bishop Sandes."

"They won't listen."

"They might. Some day they will be forced to listen, and

change." Lilith saw the pain in her brother. It may sound trite in this circumstance, she thought, but "no pain, no gain."

They were silent for a time. Robert was the first to speak. "Do you think I belong here, Lilith?"

"Yes I do, Robert. But not forever."